"I came back here because of you!"

Jonas's voice was soft, intimate. "To see if we still had a chance together."

It took all Bridget's self-control not to be swayed by his nearness. "You're a doctor, Jonas. You save lives," she answered evenly. "But not even you can breathe life into something that died ten years ago." Resolutely she turned and walked across the room.

"It isn't dead for me, Bridget." Quietly he approached from behind. His fingers brushed aside her hair, his hard mouth restamped its brand on the curve of her neck. "Is what you felt for me really dead?" he demanded huskily.

No, it's not dead, her heart cried, but she stayed silent. Jonas Concannon had hurt her once—she wouldn't trust him again!

*   *   *   *   *   *

"'Harlequin [is]...the best and the biggest.'"

—*Associated Press*
(quoting Janet Dailey's husband, Bill).

Harlequin Salutes...

JANET DAILEY

Many of these titles are available at your local bookseller.

For a free catalogue listing all available Harlequin Romances and Harlequin Presents, send your name and address to:

HARLEQUIN READER SERVICE
1440 South Priest Drive, Tempe, AZ 85281
Canadian address: Stratford, Ontario N5A 6W2

JANET DAILEY

Green Mountain Man

Harlequin Books

TORONTO • LONDON • LOS ANGELES • AMSTERDAM
SYDNEY • HAMBURG • PARIS • STOCKHOLM • ATHENS • TOKYO

First Harlequin edition published February 1979
ISBN 0-373-10272-0

This *Harlequin Salutes* edition published May 1982

Original hardcover edition published in 1978
by Mills & Boon Limited.

CHAPTER ONE

THE TIRES made a crunching sound in the crusty, packed snow along the edge of the snow-plowed road. Crossing the highway overpass, Jonas Concannon felt the grip of nostalgia at the sight of the picturesque village nestled in the valley. A patchwork of roofs rose ahead of him, the snow melting where the chimneys were perched.

The white church spire was lost against the backdrop of snow-covered mountains and fields, but Jonas located it by memory. Garlands of snow draped the trees, the full evergreens and the bare branches of the maple alike.

At the top of the small hill just before the center of town, the traffic light turned red. The car protested the forced stop on the slope of the slippery icy street.

"Nothing has changed," Jonas muttered wryly.

The light changed to green and the tires spun uselessly for seconds before finding the traction to pull the car over the top of the hill. His mouth was still twisted in the wry smile, an expression of neither gladness nor amusement, a touch of cynicism in its half-curved line, as he considered his comment.

Nothing had changed, he had said. On the surface

it seemed that way. Vermont had been covered with snow when he had left it ten years earlier. Everything in the village of Randolph appeared exactly as it had then.

"It isn't the same," Jonas declared grimly. "Not after ten years, regardless of the way it looks."

Turning onto the main street of downtown, he drove slowly across the bridge into the business district. His narrowed gray green eyes glimpsed familiar faces among the bundled figures walking along the sidewalks.

"Why did I come back?" he demanded. "Because you need a rest." He answered the question himself, and again there was the wry, twisting curve to his mouth. "And if you want any more proof of that, just keep carrying on a conversation with yourself and you'll find out how much of a rest you need, Jonas Concannon!" There was an empty parking space in front of the busy station and Jonas maneuvered the car into it. He had told Bob and Evelyn Tyler that he would drive up on Friday, but they wouldn't be expecting him until late afternoon. He had plenty of time to walk around the town and see the changes below the surface.

Snow was shoveled in a mound near the curb. He had to force the door into the snow to get his long frame out of the car. His breath formed a vapory cloud as he stepped into the chilling air and he reached back into the car for the fleece-lined jacket lying on the passenger seat.

Shrugging into it, Jonas slammed the car door and stepped over the snow pile to the sidewalk. He didn't bother to button the jacket. Instead he shoved his hands deep in the pockets to hold the front shut and began walking down the street.

Impervious to the freezing temperature and the overcast skies, he wandered aimlessly past the stores, gazing into shop windows and at the people he met. Several people he recognized, but he made no attempt to renew acquaintances.

A snowflake floated in the air before him, large and crystalline, and his hand reached out to catch it, triggered by a long-forgotten habit, something he used to do with Bridget. He stopped abruptly, the muscles working along his jawline as he stared at the white flake melting in his palm.

Face it, he told himself sternly, she's why you've come back. She is why you are wandering the streets on the off chance that you'll see her. His hand closed into a tight fist, as if to crush the snowflake and the memories it evoked.

He began walking again, more slowly, hands clenched in irritation within the pockets of his jacket. During the ten years he'd been away from Randolph, he hadn't tried to keep in touch. Not after Bob had written him that first year to tell Jonas that Bridget was married.

It was purely by accident that he'd run into Bob in Manhattan shortly before the Christmas holidays. It had been a brief reunion, with Jonas insincerely promising to come for a visit. He had never intended to come. December, January, February . . . then came March, and his resolve weakened. The pressures of work, Jonas had told himself, the need for a rest and a total change of scene no matter how brief.

The line of his mouth thinned in anger at the way he had deluded himself into believing the only reason he was returning to Randolph was for rest and relaxation. This past week when he had contacted Bob to let him know he was accepting his invitation, Jonas had carried the self-deception further by insisting no one know of his visit.

"A quiet weekend, Bob, that's all I want," Jonas had declared. "None of your parties."

"Damn!" Jonas muttered now beneath his breath, teeth clenched.

No, he hadn't wanted any parties, no chance meeting with Bridget amidst a crowd of people, no alcohol clouding his mind when he saw her again. And that was why he was here—to see Bridget again. He cursed silently in frustration, hating the inner weakness that had brought him back.

Pausing in front of a shop window, Jonas stared at his reflection framed in a pane partially steamed over. What was it the wise "they" once said? That you never quite get over your first love? Maybe he had returned to bury Bridget, he reasoned, or at least bury his image of her.

Since he had learned she had married within a year of his leaving, he had tried to imagine her with three or four kids hanging on her skirts, her slim waistline and hips gone, a frumpy housewife with rollers in her hair waiting dinner for her husband.

Jonas didn't know the man she had married. He had even blocked the man's name from his memory. But the mere thought of that stranger lying next to Bridget, touching her silky skin, sent him into a cold rage that brought a wintry frost to his gray green eyes.

A hand touched his shoulder. "Excuse me, but aren't you—"

Jonas pivoted away. "You must be mistaken," he snapped without sparing a second to identify the elderly woman.

Long, impatient strides carried him to the end of the block. Instead of crossing the street, he turned up the side street, wanting to avoid the mainstream of traffic and people and the chance that someone else might recognize him.

Slowing his steps, Jonas raked a hand through the thick tobacco brown of his hair. He breathed in deeply, filling his lungs with the cold air while trying to check the tide of impotent anger flowing through him.

"I need a drink," he muttered, nerves and muscles stretched taut.

Looking around to get his bearings, he glanced briefly at the shop nearest to him. Magnetically his gaze was drawn back, caught by the gleam of chestnut hair inside the store. Fire seared through his

9

loins, sharp and painful and white hot, his breath stolen in the shock of recognition.

It was Bridget. He'd know that face, that profile, anywhere, even blurred by the foggy-shop window. He had expected that when he saw her again after ten years, he would feel curiosity and, perhaps, the pangs of long-ago desire. Actually seeing her, he felt shaken. He hadn't anticipated this fiery leaping of the senses.

She moved, disappearing from his view. Jonas knew he had to see her more closely without the distortion of the fogged glass. Through it, she had seemed unchanged, no different than when he had left ten years ago. He didn't want that. He wanted to see her changed into a someone he no longer loved.

A bell tinkled above his head as he opened the door and walked in. Bridget's back was to the door, but she didn't turn around. Jonas paused inside, staring at her and feeling the years roll away.

A bulky pullover in forest green gave an initial impression of shapelessness until his gaze slid to the smartly tailored wool slacks of winter white she wore. The slacks revealed the slenderness of her hips and the rounded firmness of her buttocks.

Her figure hadn't changed more than an inch in ten years. She turned slightly at an angle and Jonas corrected his assessment. Not even the bulky sweater could conceal the mature fullness of her breasts jutting against the heavy knit.

Fire spread through his veins and he swore

inwardly at the desire the sight of her was arousing. It wasn't what he wanted to feel. He wanted to be indifferent, distantly amused that he had once been attracted to her. He lifted his gaze to her oval face, hardening himself against its classic beauty.

Her complexion seemed paler, the innocence gone, only the freshness remaining. There was a strained look to her mouth, a forced curve to her lips as she smiled at the woman standing in front of her. Jonas remembered the way her hazel eyes used to sparkle with a million starry lights. When he looked at them, he found them luminous and bright but lacking that fiery glitter.

It was a full second before he realized Bridget wasn't looking at the woman before her but staring beyond at something else. His gaze shifted to locate the object of her intense interest and encountered her image in a mirror placed in a corner so the shopkeeper could always see who entered the store.

Jonas realized that she had seen him almost from the instant he walked in. While he saw her reflection, Bridget saw his, the mirror locking their eyes until she sharply averted her head.

He waited for her to acknowledge him, to voice the recognition that had been in her eyes. But she gave not the slightest indication that she was even aware he was in the shop. All her attention was directed at the woman with her. The low, vibrant pitch of her voice that he remembered so well spoke only to the woman.

The impulse to force the moment of confrontation surged fiercely through him, but he checked it, steeling himself to wait. A frown creased his forehead when Bridget walked behind the cash-register counter, ringing up the sale and packaging several skeins of yarn for the woman. It struck him only then that she worked in the shop.

"Don't forget to call me when that dazzle yarn comes in, Bridget," the woman reminded her as she picked up her sack and turned toward the door.

"I won't."

At the last minute, Jonas realized he was blocking the exit and stepped to one side, nodding indifferently at the woman when she walked past him. The bell above the door dinged briefly.

All thought about Bridget working in the store vanished at the knowledge that there were only the two of them. There were no other customers. They were alone and Bridget couldn't ignore him any longer.

"Hello, Jonas."

So cool, so composed. Jonas seethed at her calmness. She could have been greeting a casual acquaintance instead of a man she had once sworn she would never stop loving. But, of course, she had stopped loving him.

That was evident by the gold wedding band she wore on her ring finger. Again, cold hatred raged in Jonas for the man who had put it there and thus became entitled to certain rights from Bridget that he couldn't claim.

"Hello, Bridget." He walked to the counter where she stood.

"You're looking well," she offered politely without extending a hand in friendly greeting.

On second thought, Jonas decided that was best. A handshake would have been a farcical gesture considering their previous relationship. He kept his hands in his pockets, an elemental tension crackling over his nerve ends.

"So are you." He returned the compliment, letting his gaze skim over her face and figure.

Alertly he saw her stiffen slightly under his deliberately intimate inspection. Just as quickly she relaxed, tipping her head to a vaguely inquiring angle.

"What brings you back to Randolph, Jonas?" she questioned.

He watched her lips form the words and their final curve into a courteous smile of interest for his answer. He remembered their softness, their responsiveness beneath the pressure of his. Passion lurked beneath her calm exterior and he knew how to arouse it.

Hadn't he been the one to awaken Bridget to the desires running latent in every woman? It was on the tip of his tongue to admit that she was the reason he had returned. Just in time, he remembered that another man had taken over the teaching of how to make love.

"I'm here visiting Bob over the weekend," he explained.

"Bob Tyler? Yes, he mentioned that he saw you before Christmas." Bridget nodded, her chestnut hair gleaming with a golden sheen from the overhead light. "He said that you'd promised to come for a visit, but I didn't think you really would."

"Didn't you? Why?" challenged Jonas, not liking the insinuation he sensed behind the remark. Regardless of the doubts he had felt at the time, events had proved he had been right to leave ten years ago.

The bell above the door chimed loudly a second before the latter was slammed shut with a force that rattled its glass. Jonas pivoted toward the sound, angered at the interruption, but the two little girls paid no attention to his icy look as they raced breathlessly past him.

"Mom, is it all right if I go over to Vicki's house?" The request was issued by the smaller of the two.

Jonas froze, his gaze narrowing on the red-cheeked girl looking earnestly at Bridget. A wisp of sandy brown hair had escaped the green-and-brown-striped stocking cap on her head, the trailing end wrapped around her neck.

The girl's brown hair was a shade lighter than Bridget's, but she had the same classic features and the same hazel eyes, the same deceptively petite build. She was Bridget's child, not necessarily a miniature of her mother, but the resemblance was obvious just the same.

"If you're certain it's all right with Vicki's mother, I don't mind." Bridget's permission was met with gleeful giggles and hurried assurances from the second girl that her mother didn't mind. "I'll pick you up at Vicki's house a little after five. You watch for me."

"I will, mom." The promise was blithely made, the girl's bubbling excitement centered on now and not later.

As the two girls turned to leave, they simultaneously noticed Jonas and paused. Youthfully bright hazel eyes studied him curiously, seemingly unaware of his intense scrutiny. Jonas kept staring, searching for the mark of her father. Finally the girl glanced hesitantly at Bridget.

"Molly, I'd like you to meet an old friend of mine, Jonas Concannon." Reluctantly the introduction was made. "Jonas, this is my daughter, Molly, and her friend Vicki Smith."

"Hello, Molly, Vicki." He nodded curtly, for some reason not trusting himself to say more.

"Hello." The breathless greeting from Molly was shyly echoed by the second girl.

"Run along, you two." Bridget smiled, and the pair darted past Jonas and out of the door with the same exuberance that marked their entrance.

Jonas watched Molly disappear before slowly bringing his gaze back to Bridget. "She looks very much like you," he commented stiffly.

"I'll—" There was a breathless catch to her voice, which Bridget self-consciously laughed off. "I'll take that as a compliment."

"I meant it as one," he confirmed. "How old is she?"

"Eight. Of course, Molly would insist that she's almost nine. It's funny how when you're young, you always want to be older."

Bridget lifted a hand to flip her shoulder-length hair away from the rolled collar of her pullover, the first gesture of nervousness Jonas had seen her make. There was a measure of satisfaction in knowing she wasn't as poised and nonchalant as she appeared.

He hoped he was making her uncomfortable. He knew what she was doing to him. God, how he knew! He thrust his hands deeper in his pockets, balling them into fists.

"Do you have any more children?" The question was dragged from his throat while over and over his mind kept repeating, "Molly could have been ours."

"Only Molly. She's happy and healthy, and I'm satisfied with that." Bridget forced a smile, the corners of her mouth trembling with the effort.

Jonas wondered if she, too, was thinking that Molly could have been their child. But she wasn't. Another man had fathered her, and Jonas felt the bitter swell of jealousy and anger.

"How are your parents?" He changed the subject abruptly.

"Very well." Her hazel eyes didn't quite meet his look as she answered. "It's coming into the busy time for them with sap starting to run. You wouldn't recognize the sugar-bush. Dad has pipes running all over now. It's much more efficient than bucketing it out in sleds."

"Genuine Vermont maple syrup." Jonus tipped his head back, remembering. "It's been years since I've had any."

Not in ten years. But it was eleven years ago that Jonas was recalling. He had volunteered to help Bridget and her father gather the sap one weekend. Once the sap started running it was a daily chore and he had taken part on that one occasion.

Jonas remembered tramping through the wet snow to the large grove of maple trees on the farm with Bridget at his side, a gloved hand clasped in his. Her father had walked behind the sled pulled by the Morgan mare, the bells on the harness jingling in the crisp air.

The sky was sharply blue, the sun brilliant and the barren branches of the maple trees had cast cobwebby shadows on the snow. It was all so fresh in his mind that it could have been yesterday.

"The maple trees have to be about forty years old, then it takes four of them to make a barrel of sap." Jonas began mimicking the lecture Bridget's father had given him as if he'd been a city boy. "And it takes a barrel of sap to make one gallon of maple syrup. You don't make it into syrup by snapping your fingers. No, sir, you have to boil it down to a thick consistency, testing until you get it to the exact density. Then it has to be filtered and graded, packed and labeled. It's a science."

Bringing his chin level again, he gazed at Bridget, a gentle smile softening the hard line of his mouth. "Do you remember that day?"

"How could I forget?" The firelights were back in her eyes, dancing and laughing, caught in the magic spell of memory. "You bombarded me with snowballs."

"Strictly in self-defense. You kept shoving snow down my neck," Jonas reminded her.

His gaze slid to her lips, parted in a ruefully acknowledging smile at the way she had provoked him those many years ago. The snowballs had only been a part of his retaliation. The rest had come when Bridget lost her footing in the snow and had fallen while trying to run from him.

She had laid there laughing, too breathless to move, and he had joined her in the bed of snow, intending only to silence her with a kiss. No, that wasn't true. He had wanted to make love to her, whether it had been in the middle of a blizzard or on the rim of an erupting volcano.

But the first kiss had been innocent enough until Bridget had seen the veiled look in his eyes and had made an almost inaudible moan of surrender. There had been nothing innocent in the second kiss, nor the third or fourth. Jonas remembered fighting through her heavy winter outergarments to find the slender, feminine form they hid.

Only there hadn't been any satisfaction in that. He had wanted to feel the warm softness of her flesh, but her father had called to them, the mare's jingling harness warning them of his approach. One glance and her father had known more had happened than a playful romp in the snow, but he had said nothing.

It had been the first of many times that Bridget had driven Jonas to the edge of his control. There had been moments when he was certain she enjoyed making him insane with wanting her.

It had been the beginning. But where there is a beginning, there must also be an end. Jonas thought it had ended, until now, this moment, when he wanted her more than he ever had in the past.

Tearing his gaze from her trembling lips, he saw that Bridget felt it, too. It was there in the darkening of her hazel eyes, the sweet torment of physical wanting.

"Bridget." His low, husky voice said her name in urgent demand.

She looked away, drawing a deep breath and releasing it in a shuddering sigh. "That was a long time ago, Jonas."

"Was it?" he issued tautly, angered that she could control her emotions when he had so little control over his.

"I . . . have a customer coming. Excuse me." Except for that second's hesitation, Bridget was again cool and composed.

Flicking an impatient glance toward the door, Jonas saw the woman a step away from the entrance. He turned instantly back to Bridget, his look hard and demanding. "Send her away," he ordered. "Tell her you're closing early today."

The stubborn set of her chin gave him his answer before she spoke. "I won't do that, Jonas," she said quietly. "Not can't, but won't."

The shop door opened and closed to the tinkling of the overhead bell. "Hi, Bridget. It looks like snow out there. Have you heard the forecast?" the woman asked, dabbing a tissue against her red and runny nose. She nodded briefly at Jonas, giving him a curious look.

"No, I haven't," Bridget denied.

"It's going to snow," the woman insisted, then glanced around the store. "Where's your jute?"

Jonas shifted in irritation, wishing the woman would find her jute and get out. He studied Bridget's composed features while she pointedly ignored him.

"It's in the aisle behind the dark skeins of yarn. What are you looking for?" she inquired, and Jonas gritted his teeth.

"I don't know." The woman shrugged, reaching in her pocket for a slip of paper. "I'm picking it up for my sister Bonnie. She wrote down what she wanted. This craft stuff is her thing, not mine."

"I'll help you." Bridget stepped from behind the counter as the woman behind the aisle.

Jonas turned to block her path, catching her by the shoulders to stop her when she would have pushed her way past him. She stiffened in resistance, flashing him a resentful look.

"Have dinner with me tonight." The invitation was halfway between a command and a plea. He wasn't content to just hold her as his fingers began to sensually massage her shoulders. "For old times' sake."

The impulse was there to draw her against his chest and kiss her into a submissive mood of acceptance, but Jonas couldn't do that, not after ten years, and not after the circumstances of his leaving, regardless of what the interim had proved.

"It isn't possible, Jonas." Bridget coldly and firmly removed his hands from her shoulders. Smiling aloofly, she added, "Have a good time this weekend. I know Bob and Evelyn will enjoy your visit."

In final dismissal, she brushed past him. The gold of her wedding band winked mockingly from her left hand and Jonas cursed himself for forgetting its presence. Rigidly he watched her disappear behind the aisle without a backward glance.

He was a fool to come back. It had been over ten years since he had left, and the ashes were cold. It was too late to breathe fire into them now, especially when another man had built one in his place.

Jonas stormed out of the shop, slamming the door in frustration. Why had he let her creep back into his system like a recurring sickness? Why couldn't ten years have made her fat and misshapen or dowdy and frigid?

He was halfway to his car before the mountain air

cooled his temper and slowed his stride. The ignition keys were in his hand and he was reaching for the door when he glimpsed the skis on top of his car.

With split second decision, he turned away to enter the bus depot-drugstore combination. He walked directly to the pay telephone and thumbed through the directory until he found the number he was looking for. Dropping the coins in the slot, he dialed the number and waited.

A man answered and Jonas spoke briskly. "Hello, Bob, this is Jonas."

"Jonas! Evie has the spare room all ready for you and dinner in the oven. Where are you?" There was a brief pause before he added, "Evie said if your car has broken down, she doesn't want to hear about it. No excuse will be accepted for missing dinner tonight."

"Look, I'm sorry, Bob," Jonas broke in impatiently, "but something's come up. I can't make it."

"You don't expect me to believe that, do you?" Bob laughed. "What is she? Blond or brunette? I know—brunette, that sexy little number I saw you with in New York!"

Jonas neither confirmed nor denied that there was a woman involved in his decision. "Let me take a raincheck on your invitation, Bob, and I'll visit another time," he lied.

"You're always welcome, you know that."

"You have my telephone number. If you ever get back to New York, call me," he offered politely.

"Maybe next month. Evie has been talking about going ever since I left her out of my pre-Christmas trip. Take care and don't do anything I wouldn't do."

A few minutes later, Jonas was behind the wheel driving out of town. Maybe I'll call Eileen when I get back, he thought disinterestedly. I haven't seen her for a while.

With a start he realized he hadn't seen the brunette Bob had mentioned since he had made up his mind three weeks ago he was coming to Vermont this weekend. Bridget's memory had been working on him as early as then.

"Damn!" His fist hit the steering wheel in frustration.

CHAPTER TWO

TOWELING THE BATH WATER from her skin, Bridget
paused uncertainly, listening. Someone was moving
around in the living room. Draping the towel over a
hook, she reached for the cotton robe hanging on the
bathroom door. The material clung to her damp skin,
interfering with her efforts to pull it around her.

She ventured into the small hallway, tying the sash
as she walked. The living room was empty when she
peered around the corner, but she heard movement
in the kitchen. Pushing the hair away from her
forehead, she frowned.

"Who's there?" she called, moving hesitantly
toward the open archway to the kitchen.

A dark-haired woman moved into her view,
smiling and waving to her from the area near the
kitchen sink. "It's just me."

"Mother!" Bridget sighed in exasperation. "What
are you doing?"

"I brought over some scallions and lettuce from
the garden. It really makes a difference to start the
plants in the greenhouse first. Do you know I believe
we will have tomatoes ripe enough to eat next week?
I do enjoy fresh vegetables and your father just loves

working with plants." She began opening cupboard doors. "I brought over some roses, too. Where do you keep your vases, Bridget? I really think you should start locking your door. Living alone the way you do in the country and with new people moving in all the time, you just never know who might walk in."

"That's true," Bridget agreed dryly, and walked to the cupboard above the stove to get the vase.

"Oh! You were taking a bath!" Margaret Harrison declared, only that moment noticing the robe her daughter wore and the damp tendrils of chestnut hair around her neck.

"Yes, mother." Bridget was accustomed to her mother's lack of observation.

"Are you going out tonight?" She began arranging the roses in the vase Bridget had handed her.

"Yes, with Jim," Bridget replied, with a lilt to her voice that prodded the memory of a previous instance when she had related her plans for the evening. "I can arrange the flowers."

"Yes, you do that," her mother agreed, "and I'll clean the lettuce and the scallions."

"There's no need for you to do that, mother." Bridget determinedly stayed calm. "I will."

"You're going out this evening. You can't have your hands smelling like scallions." She turned the cold water tap on in the sink. "Where do you keep your knives, Bridget?" Counting to ten, Bridget opened the silverware drawer and handed a paring knife to her mother. "I should think it would be much easier if you kept the knives in a separate drawer. There's too much risk of accidentally cutting yourself when they're with other utensils. But it's your house and you're entitled to keep them where you please."

"Thank you, mother." But the faintly caustic remark sailed right over her mother's head.

"Jim is a good man. I like him," Margaret Harrison continued, not missing the beat. "He'd make an excellent father for Molly. Strong and dependable, intelligent, too. He isn't still working on that highway crew during the summers, is he?"

"Yes, mother." Bridget tried to concentrate on the roses.

"That's such a shame. He should spend the summers furthering his education instead of wasting such a fine mind doing manual labor," was the sighing reply.

"Jim is still trying to pay for the cost of his first education," Bridget pointed out dryly.

"Of course, I understand that," her mother nodded, but Bridget doubted that she did. "But I just know that he could do so much better than teaching in this little college. I—"

"The Technical College in Randolph Center is an excellent school," Bridget defended.

"Yes, but Jim could do better. With a little more training, I'm sure he could get a professorship in some Ivy League college, Princeton or Dartmouth. It would be so much better for you and Molly."

"Mother, isn't anybody good enough for me as they are?" Bridget demanded, agitated beyond endurance by her mother's constant meddling. "Must you keep trying to change them and mold them into what you think they should be?"

"I am not trying to interfere." Margaret Harrison looked sincerely stunned by the accusation. "Your father and I only want what's best for you."

"Don't bring dad into it," Bridget protested. "You know very well he only thinks and says what you tell him."

"You know very well we talk things over—"

"Until he finally agrees with what you decide." Bridget turned away. She was losing her temper, and it was pointless.

"I assure you, Bridget, in everything we do we always first try to think what would be best for you. And that includes the men you see. We want you to have the best, and that isn't wrong," her mother smiled. "Molly is going to be getting to that age soon and you'll find out for yourself what your father and I have gone through with you. Speaking of Molly, where is she? Out riding?"

"No, she's been wanting to spend the night with Vicki ever since the summer vacation started. Since I was going out with Jim, tonight seemed the perfect opportunity."

"Vicki? The Smith girl? Really, Bridget, do you think that association is—"

"Mother!" Bridget pressed a hand to her forehead,

rubbing at the throbbing pain of tension. "She is my daughter. I am quite capable of deciding whom she should have as friends. Just the way you decided for me ten years ago!"

Her mother stared at her for a silent moment, a hurt look to her brown eyes. "Why in heaven's name would you bring that up?"

"I don't know," Bridget shrugged impatiently. Her hand was shaking as she reached to adjust the roses in the vase. She felt the familiar hollow, gnawing pain eating at her chest. "It doesn't matter."

Her mother turned back to the sink, rinsing the lettuce under the tap. "Your father and I were certainly proved right to do what we did. After all—"

"But maybe I didn't want you to be right." Bridget had to press a hand to her mouth to help swallow back a sob. "Maybe I loved him. Maybe that's all I cared about." She ran her fingers through her hair. "Didn't you ever think of that?"

"It's all in the past, Bridget. You shouldn't let it upset you anymore. You have Jim now and—"

"I don't happen to love Jim," she retorted stiffly. "He's very nice and good fun, but it ends there. So don't go planning any wedding in the future. One was enough."

"You surely can't be feeling bitter about that," her mother protested with a disbelieving frown. "You have Molly and—"

"Mother, please, go home." Bridget reached over and turned off the cold water. "I don't mean to hurt

28

your feelings, but I would like you to leave before I lose my temper."

"If that's what you want—" Margaret Harrison's chin elevated in stiff acceptance, wounded dignity in her proud smile "—of course I'll leave."

She carefully dried her hands on a terry towel near the sink and Bridget felt the emotional guilt swarming over her.

"Oh, mother," she sighed, "it's not that I don't understand. I know you love me, but I'm twenty-eight years old. I have my own home and my own family now. I have to live my own life and make my own mistakes. You can't keep treating me like a child and trying to run my life."

"I am not trying to run your life, but I can't stop thinking of you as my daughter."

"I will always be your daughter," Bridget agreed patiently. "The only difference is that I'm an adult. Please give me some credit for having a little common sense and intelligence."

"I do—I always have," her mother insisted.

"Have you? Is that why ten years ago—"

"Ten years ago you were too blinded by romantic dreams to see anything for yourself," Margaret reproved sharply. "And ten years ago I proved that he was not the man for you. I don't understand why you keep harping back to the same subject."

Bridget turned away. It was not something she could discuss with her mother. "I have to get dressed. Jim will be here in a few minutes."

As she started toward the bedroom, her mother asked, "Where are the two of you going tonight? Didn't you say something about a show in Montpelier?"

"That's where we were going originally, but Jim called this afternoon to change it." Her response was automatic.

"Where are you going?"

Bridget stopped, her mouth opening in a silent laugh born of anger and disbelief. "Didn't you hear a word I said earlier, mother?" she asked. "I don't have to account to you for my whereabouts."

"Someone should know where you'll be in case something should happen to Molly and we would need to get a hold of you," Margaret reasoned.

Shaking her head, Bridget didn't argue. Sometimes it was easier to give in than to fight for every scrap of her independence.

"Bob and Evelyn Tyler are having a party tonight. We're going there," she sighed. "Mrs. Smith knows where she can reach me."

"The Tylers?" Her mother's mouth curved in an expression of distaste. "Their parties can be such rowdy affairs."

"They're good clean fun. Noisy sometimes," Bridget admitted, "but remember, mother, we live in Vermont where the trees are close together and the people are far apart. Run along home. Dad will be wondering where you are."

"What's the occasion? For the party, I mean."

Margaret typically ignored what she didn't want to hear.

"There isn't any occasion—just some friends getting together on a Saturday night. Now I have to get dressed." Again she started toward the bedroom.

"What time will you be home?"

Bridget stopped, angry sparks flashing in her eyes. "I have no idea." She looked over her shoulder in challenge. "Maybe I won't come home," she threatened falsely. "Maybe I'll find an orgy going on somewhere and have Jim take me to it instead!"

"Bridget!" her mother breathed in shocked astonishment. She found nothing funny about the false threat.

"You'd better leave. Because, so help me, if you're still here when Jim comes, I'll start locking the door and I'll make sure you don't have a key!"

"I don't know what's the matter with you, Bridget, but you've certainly been short-tempered lately," Margaret declared indignantly.

The bedroom door banged against its frame as Bridget angrily shut it behind her. Immediately she stopped, breathing a silent laugh. The bedroom-door-slamming scene was an often-repeated one, a part of her childhood she hadn't left behind. It was a childish display of temper. At twenty-eight, Bridget had become convinced that no one grows up. They only become inhibited.

As for the shortness of her temper, she knew the reason for that, too, and her preoccupation with the past. It was a direct result of that Friday in March when Jonas had stopped at the store. When she'd seen him standing outside, she had nearly gone to pieces.

Fortunately, Mrs. Dutton had kept rattling on about something. When he'd walked into the store, she couldn't make up her mind whether to run to him or from him. She had done neither.

All in all, Bridget thought she had handled the meeting fairly well, appearing calm and poised regardless of the emotional turmoil that had been going on inside. There had been a couple of bad moments. In the end, she had kept her pride intact and brushed him off.

Previously she had been convinced that, although she hadn't forgotten him, he had become just an unpleasant memory. Bridget had really begun to believe she could have a happy and rewarding life without Jonas.

But seeing him again had brought back all the love and passion she had felt, and all the searing hurt she had known ten years ago. It wasn't easy reliving it again and going through the agony of getting over him a second time. She would, of course, and maybe this time it wouldn't take as long.

In the meantime, Jim would be arriving any second. Vermont's merry widow, he called her. Bridget was determined that tonight she would be just that, without any memories of the past to haunt her.

The merriest person at the party would be Bridget O'Shea, widow of the late Brian O'Shea. Walking to her closet, she began to search for an outfit that would match her new mood.

Twenty minutes later a male voice called out, "Hello? Anybody home?"

"I'll be right out, Jim," Bridget answered, taking a last-minute look in the mirror, fluffing the sides of her hair with her fingers before leaving the bedroom. "How do I look?"

She made a brief pirouette before the man standing in front of the sliding-glass doors. Medium height, on the stocky side, with dark hair, Jim studied her appreciatively through his dark-rimmed glasses.

"Like a blast of sunshine." A lazy grin spread across his face, the ready smile one of the most appealing things about him, as he ran an appraising eye over her slender, slacks-clad figure.

"Too bright, is it?" Bridget laughed, glancing down at her slacks.

The plaid of her slacks was in shades of yellow, predominantly canary, with a thin red stripe for out-line contrast. The short-sleeved knit top with a scooped neckline was white with a large flower of the plaid material appliqued in the front.

"It looks great," Jim assured her in a voice that said he had only been kidding before.

"Will I need a jacket, do you think?" She hesi-tated.

"That depends on whether or not you were

planning to take a moonlight stroll with me around midnight." His fingers curled an imaginary moustache.

"Seriously, Jim." Bridget smiled with affectionate exasperation.

"I was serious." He lifted his shoulders in an expressive shrug and sighed. "But you're not."

"Come on—" she refused to let the conversation shift to their personal relationship "—should I take a jacket or not?"

"Probably should," Jim answered at last. "It's hard telling how much of the party will be outside and how much in. It could get chilly after the sun goes down."

"I'll take my windbreaker," Bridget decided. "I think it's in the kitchen."

"Hurry up," he prompted as she started toward the kitchen. "I volunteered to bring a keg of beer and I don't want it to get warm before we get to Bob's."

The jacket was draped over the back of the chair near the breakfast table. "Here it is." Bridget folded it over her arm and turned to rejoin Jim.

Her attention was caught by the spotless sink, not a trace of lettuce or scallions in sight. She looked for the roses and saw the vase sitting on the coffee table in the living room, rearranged into a more attractive grouping than she had done.

"Of all the—" She snapped her teeth shut on the rest of the angry ejaculation. "I don't believe it."

"Don't believe what?" Jim asked curiously. "Why the frown? What's wrong?"

"Nothing," she breathed heavily. "It's just my mother, tidying up after me."

"My mother is the same way. Irritating, isn't it?" he agreed with a smile. "Ready?" He opened the sliding-glass door onto the porch of the chalet for her. "It can't be easy living across the road from your parents, still under their thumb, so to speak."

Bridget flicked a brief glance at the big white house opposite her small chalet. "That's putting it mildly at times," she replied and walked beside Jim to his small Datsun wagon. "I think my mother spends as much time taking care of my house as she does her own."

"Not everybody can have free maid service," Jim said, looking at the bright side as he opened the passenger door of the car for Bridget.

She smiled in rueful acceptance of his attempt. "True. I guess it really isn't too bad. And I certainly can't say that I didn't know what my neighbors would be like before I moved in here."

"Now you have the idea," he smiled and walked around the car to the driver's side.

"It was especially convenient when Molly was younger," Bridget enlarged on the statement. "I didn't have to worry about her coming home from school and not having anyone here because I was working. All she had to do was walk across the road to grandma's until I came."

"Molly's a bright kid," Jim commented idly as he reversed out of the driveway. "Is she staying over there tonight?"

"No, she's spending the night with a girl friend, much to mother's dismay," she sighed. "My mother is a snob."

"Your mother is a do-gooder like mine," he corrected. "She always does what she thinks is right and proper for somebody else, regardless of that somebody else's opinion, and makes enemies instead of grateful friends."

"Did you say you were a psychology professor?" Bridget laughed.

"No, I just know my mother. And from what you've told me about yours, they could be related," he grinned.

"You're very good for me, Jim." She leaned back in the seat, relaxing, no longer upset by her mother's interference.

"I could be better, but we won't go into that," he added quickly when his sliding glance saw Bridget tense. "Patience is one of my main virtues, as you'll discover."

"And perception," she added thoughtfully.

"It doesn't take much perception to see that you were deeply hurt when you lost your husband," Jim shrugged.

She looked out the window at the vividly green landscape. "Brian was a good man, compassionate and understanding. You're like him in many ways."

"Is that why you're so wary? The good don't always die young, Bridget," he teased, but with a note of seriousness.

"I know," she agreed, nodding faintly without letting her gaze wander from the countryside. "It's all so green, isn't it?"

Jim studied her profile for a second, knowing she had deliberately changed the subject, but as he had said, he was patient. Six months ago, she had refused to go out with him. He had made progress since then.

"Like an emerald jewel," he commented.

It was only a few minutes' drive to the Tyler house. Of course, any place in Vermont seemed to be only a short drive away through unspoiled countryside. Rolling hills and jutting mountains were covered with trees in every shade of green—pines, maples, and birch. Verdant meadows and fields dotted the valleys, rustic and beautiful with occasional stone-wall fences meandering through them.

A stand of white birch marked the front lawn of the Tyler house. There were already several cars in the driveway when Jim pulled in. The sounds of laughing voices and music indicated the party had begun.

"I think everyone's in the backyard," Jim observed. "You go ahead and I'll get the keg of beer from the back."

"All right." Bridget smiled, stepping out of the car when he switched off the engine.

She had barely rounded the corner of the house when she was hailed with a chorus of greetings. A half a dozen couples had already arrived. Hamburgers were sizzling on the grills set up near the picnic tables in the backyard. One table was already laden with an assortment of other foods for a buffet.

"It's about time you came. We were going to eat without you," Bob threatened laughingly.

"No, you wouldn't," Bridget countered, "Jim is bringing the beer."

At that moment, Jim rounded the corner, toting the keg of beer on his shoulder. Thirsty volunteers gave him a hand in setting it down and breaking it open. With good-natured jostling, they argued over who would draw the first draft.

Evelyn emerged from the rear entrance of the house, pot holders offering a protective grip for the handles of the hot dish she was carrying. She started to greet Bridget, but didn't complete it.

"Bob!" she wailed in protest. "You were supposed to be watching the hamburgers!"

"Sorry." Bob, tall and dark with a waistline that was beginning to thicken, raced to the smoking grills. "I hope everybody wants their hamburgers well-done," he joked as he began the rescue efforts.

"He's worse than a child," Evelyn murmured to Bridget with a rueful shake of her head. "You can't turn your back on him for a minute."

"Can I help with something?" Bridget asked.

"You can fix the relish tray. Everything is in the refrigerator and the dish is on the counter," her hostess suggested.

The barbecue parties the Tyler's gave were always informal gatherings with everyone lending a hand. It was almost a family affair. Most of the couples had known each other since school days.

"Consider it done." Bridget started toward the house.

"Keep the cat out of the jelly, will you?" Evelyn called after her. "I don't know what he thinks it is, but he's fascinated by it."

"Will do." She laughed the promise.

The pumpkin-colored tomcat was crouched on a kitchen chair when Bridget entered the house. An unmolded jellied salad, the object of the cat's interest, was sitting on the table. His tail swished in resentment as she shooed it from the chair before walking to the refrigerator.

Humming softly to herself, she began setting out the celery, carrot sticks and various other ingredients she found and began arranging them on the partitioned plate. As she was spooning olives from the jar, she heard footsteps enter the kitchen from another room of the house. Anticipating one of the three Tyler children, she didn't bother to look.

"Hello, Bridget."

The spoon of olives halted in midair. For an instant she couldn't breathe. Her gaze darted to the man pausing beside her to lean a shoulder against the refrigerator door. First searing fire, then ice ran through her veins.

"Hello, Jonas." Was that her voice responding so calmly? "I see you've finally managed to accept Bob's invitation for a visit."

Her hand was amazingly steady as it carried the

spoon to the relish tray, but she was painfully aware of him standing beside her. The clean male scent of him filled her senses.

His hair glistened damply as if he had recently stepped from the shower, darkening its normal golden brown shade. A white shirt was opened at the throat, its long sleeves rolled halfway up his forearms. A pair of crisp new Levi's covered his long legs.

"Yes. I canceled my March visit." Jonas reached past her to steal an olive. "But I imagine you know that," he added dryly.

"Evelyn mentioned you'd called at the last minute to postpone it," Bridget admitted. It would have been useless to deny it.

"And you didn't say anything about seeing me." It was a statement, not really needing any confirmation.

"I didn't see the point." She added more olives to the tray. "They were already disappointed that you hadn't come. I know they must be delighted to have you here now."

There was room for more radishes, but Bridget didn't bother with them. She wanted to get out of the house and become insulated from Jonas's presence by the crowd outside.

"You aren't," Jonas stated.

"I'm not what?" She screwed the lid on the olive jar, avoiding his gaze as she had since he had appeared.

"Delighted that I'm here now," he mocked.

"Of course I am," she lied brightly.

"That's funny. You don't look it," Jonas observed dryly, tipping his head slightly to get a better view of her expression.

"I'm sorry you think that." Bridget shrugged and picked up the relish tray. As she turned to leave, Jonas moved as if intending to keep her from going. "Would you bring the jellied salad from the table when you come? I think we're just about ready to eat."

His brooding gray green eyes studied her seemingly composed features for a disturbing second before he walked to the table. Bridget knew he was right behind her when she left the house.

"Finally the guest of honor arrives!" Bob declared when he saw Jonas following her. He lifted his glass of beer in a toast. "Welcome home, Jonas!"

Evidently this was Jonas's first appearance at the party, Bridget guessed, as the other couples gathered around to greet him. Placing the relish tray with the other food dishes, Bridget walked to the charcoal grills where Evelyn had replaced Bob as the chef.

"Let me hold the platter," she offered, taking the oblong flat dish that Evelyn was trying to balance while lifting the patties from the grill with a long-handled spatula.

It was surrendered willingly. "Jonas is receiving a hero's welcome, isn't he?" Evelyn spared a brief glance in the direction of the main group.

"He certainly is!"

The hint of sharpness in Bridget's voice didn't go unnoticed. She realized it when she saw the flicker of concern in Evelyn's green eyes.

"You don't mind about Jonas being here, do you?" she asked. "After Bob asked you and Jim, I wondered if it would bother you. The two of you broke up so suddenly. None of us had ever known exactly what went wrong. You left so soon after Jonas did."

"No, I don't mind," Bridget rushed in to assure her. "It all happened ten years ago."

"I'm glad you feel that way." Her hostess sighed in relief.

The truth was that it seemed like only yesterday. Bridget's gaze wandered to Jonas, haunting memories clouding her eyes. The first time she'd seen him eleven years ago she thought he looked like a mountain man, tall and rugged, standing an inch over six feet.

Well muscled, without an ounce of spare flesh, he gave an erroneous appearance of leanness. His wide chest and shoulders tapered to slim waist and hips. There had been something primitive and dangerous about him then, an earthy maleness that was virilely lethal.

Ten years hadn't made any changes in his appearance, except that he looked harder, more cynical and more arrogantly aloof now. A veneer of sophistication covered the set of his ruggedly hewn features, but Jonas was still charismatic. He would still be noticed in a crowd.

Watching him, Bridget saw him laugh, the slashed lines deepening around his mouth, his eyes crinkling at the corners. She remembered the potency of his smile that could disarm the wariest of hearts, including her own. Ten years hadn't changed that, either.

"Ah, food!" Jim was standing beside her, sniffing hungrily at the platter of meat. Possessively he curved an arm around her waist. "You and I are going to be first in line to eat."

Bridget was about to make some idle response when Jonas swung a harsh, narrowed look at her. She discovered another thing about him that hadn't changed. His alert gaze never missed anything.

He still possessed that uncanny knack of always knowing where she was and who she was with even when he seemed not to be aware of her. It was disconcerting to learn that this invisible link hadn't weakened.

More than that, she knew Jonas still wanted her, but she wouldn't fall into that trap a second time. Deliberately she beamed an adoring and happy smile at Jim, knowing Jonas would see it and draw his own conclusions. She was sorry if Jim mistook her meaning, but more than ever before she needed him to stay close to her tonight, a shield to ward off Jonas.

CHAPTER THREE

JONAS DIDN'T MAKE any attempt to test the durability of her shield, not even approaching Bridget while she was in Jim's company. The setting of the sun brought out the mosquitoes and the party was forced to continue inside.

The close quarters of the living room-dining room combination made it impossible for Bridget to avoid Jonas indefinitely. When she saw him wandering toward the sofa where she and Jim were seated, she braced herself for the inevitable conversation. Unfortunately, Bob chose that moment to refill his beer glass, leaving a chair vacant beside the sofa.

"Mind if I sit down?" By the time the entire question was spoken, Jonas was already sitting in the empty chair.

"I don't," Bridget lied, striving for the light note, "but Bob might when he comes back. He was sitting there."

"I'll fight with him over it." Jonas smiled lazily, the glittering light in his eyes mocking her denial before sliding to Jim. His arm was draped over the back of the sofa near Bridget's shoulders.

"Have you met Jim Spencer?" An introduction seemed necessary. "He teaches at the college."

"And survives the summers doing road construction," Jim inserted before Bridget could say any more. He offered a hand to Jonas. "We met informally outside."

"Yes, I remember," Jonas nodded in apparent friendliness.

But Bridget saw the assessing gleam that measured his opponent, a suggestion of animal cunning in the look. Muscles flexed in his tanned forearm as Jonas briefly gripped Jim's hand. Then he leaned back, relaxing in the chair. Yet Bridget guessed that he was no more relaxed than she was, her nerves jumping, alert to every move he made or didn't make.

A stereo was playing in the far corner of the room. The couples had scattered into clusters in various parts of the room, milling around changing groups, laughing and talking, enjoying themselves as Bridget wished she could.

"Bob's parties haven't changed since we went to them together, have they, Bridget?" Jonas seemed to casually toss out the observation.

Bridget tensed. She hadn't mentioned anything to Jim about Jonas. Prior to the party, it hadn't seemed necessary, since she hadn't wanted to call attention to the fact that she had an old boyfriend present.

"You two used to know one another?" The possiblity hadn't seemed to occur to Jim until that moment.

Her gaze ricocheted from his curious look and was encountered and caught by the cynically amused light in Jonas's eyes. The hard line of his mouth twitched slightly.

"Bridget and I knew each other very well," Jonas answered.

Her cheeks flamed at his dryly suggestive tone, the heat spreading through every inch of her body. Jim's arm slid down to her shoulders, firmly staking the claim he hadn't thought necessary a moment ago.

"That was a long time ago, Jonas," she breathed in resentment, flashing him an angry look.

"So you said before," he returned with a glint of skepticism that said time had no bearing on the matter.

Considering the havoc he was raising with her senses, Bridget was afraid he was right and she didn't want him to be. His gaze flicked to the empty glass in her hand.

"Would you like me to refill that for you?" Jonas offered.

"Yes, please," Bridget answered. Her eagerness was to have him gone.

"I'll get it for you." Jim reached for the glass she had started to hand to Jonas. His air was definitely proprietorial, stating that *he* took care of Bridget's needs, not Jonas.

Shrugging an acceptance of Jim's claim, Jonas didn't argue, and Bridget couldn't protest. Only when Jim was walking away did she notice the satisfied curve to his mouth that said Jonas had known what Jim's reaction would be. He had been left alone with her the way he had planned. Her shield had been disposed of and Bridget was vulnerable.

"Afraid?" Jonas challenged in a treacherously low voice.

"Of what?" Her hazel eyes were deliberately blank and innocent.

"Of being alone with me," he explained, even though the glint in his eyes said he knew it was unnecessary.

"Don't be silly, Jonas," she said, angered that he could sense her reaction.

His jaw tightened, a mask stealing over his face to make his expression unreadable. He lowered his gaze to the amber liquid in the glass in his hand.

"Why didn't you tell me your husband was dead, Bridget?" he demanded.

Unconsciously, she turned the plain gold band on her finger, a nervous, protective reaction to his sudden change of the subject.

"I assumed you knew," she answered truthfully. "It's common knowledge to everyone here that Brian is dead."

"I didn't know until Bob mentioned it." There was an impatient snap to his answer, followed by an equally sharp glance. "You don't seem too grief stricken."

"Brian has been dead a long time. You can't expect me to wear black the rest of my life," Bridget defended herself, bridling at his implied censure.

Again he let his gaze concentrate on the beer in his glass. "Did you love him?"

"That doesn't deserve an answer," she hissed in pain and anger, nearly choking from the tightness in her throat, "not if you think I would let a man father my child without loving him."

Jonas glanced at her but seemed otherwise unaffected by her indignant outburst. If anything, he appeared dubious of its roots.

"I suppose you loved him as much as you claimed to love me?" Although it was spoken smoothly, there was a sarcastic bite to the question.

"No," Bridget retorted in kind. "I didn't demean myself twice."

"Where did you meet this Brian—" Jonas waited for her to fill in the blank.

"O'Shea, Brian O'Shea," she obliged and hesitated. There was no reason not to answer his question. Anyone in the room could tell him the story. "After you—left, mother thought I should get away for a while, so I went to stay with her sister in Pittsburgh. Brian was her husband's nephew."

"Ah, yes, mother," he jeered contemptuously. "I suppose she approved of Brian."

"Yes. He was a good man, gentle and understanding, two things I needed very desperately at the time." Without realizing it, Bridget had got to her feet, unable to continue the conversation.

Fluidly Jonas rose to stop her, his fingers lightly circling her waist, his touch paralyzing her. "I know you were hurt when I left," he admitted roughly, "but it didn't leave any lasting scars."

Didn't it? Look at my heart, she wanted to cry. But Bridget kept silent, preferring to let him believe that she had got over him whether it was true or not.

"So what happened? How did—Brian die?" he growled the name savagely, almost in jealous hatred.

"In a car crash. Instantly." The words were clipped and to the point.

"And you went running home to mama," Jonas concluded in a faint sneer.

"Within a few months, yes." Her chin lifted to a proud angle, but she didn't let her gaze rise to meet his. "It isn't easy to cope when you're young and alone and have a small child. And I was homesick for Vermont. I didn't like the city."

"This Jim fellow? What is he to you?" His fingers tightened punishingly around her wrist, threatening to cut off the circulation to enforce his demand.

"Does it matter?" Bridget protested, darting him an angry look.

"Dammit, yes!" An irritated frown creased his forehead as if he regretted admitting it. At the wary light in her eyes, he gave a little groan and swore beneath his breath. "For God's sake, let's dance."

"No."

But he was already propelling her to an empty space in the living room and turning her into his arms. Bridget couldn't object without creating a scene. Besides, she was certain if she protested too strongly Jonas would suspect how susceptible she still was to him.

The firm hand at the back of her waist forced her to dance close to him, the muscular hardness of his thighs brushing against hers. Bridget stared at the open collar of his shirt, fighting the dizzying sensation of being in his arms again.

Her hand rested lightly on his shoulder as she tried not to feel the warmth of his flesh burning through the white of his shirt. His hand began to roam slowly and familiarly over her lower back and spine, her bones melting into marshmallow sticks. When Jonas bent his head, she had to close her eyes as his breath stirred the hair along her neck.

"We'll start fresh, Bridget," he stated.

"No." She shook her head, trying to sound as determined as he did.

"Why not? You want to—I can feel it." There was no mistaking the confidence in his tone.

"No, I don't, Jonas," she insisted tightly. "If—If I've given you that impression, then it's only because I'm susceptible to memories, too, remembering the way it used to be."

"It doesn't have to be just memories. I still want you, Bridget," he admitted in demand.

"No," she breathed, "you only want a weekend fling with an old flame."

His mouth moved against her hair, sending tremors quaking through her limbs. "I want more than that."

"You . . . you can't come waltzing back into my life after ten years and expect to take up where you left off," Bridget protested.

"I will," Jonas replied decisively, his head bending lower as he searched for the sensitive area along the curve of her neck.

His self-assurance bordered on arrogance. It was the prod Bridget needed to remember more than her love. It reminded her of why he had left ten years ago. Her hands strained against his chest wedging a space between them.

"No, Jonas." Her voice was cold and positive. It, more than her resistance, stopped him. "Ten years ago you said goodbye to me. Now it's my turn. I don't care if I ever see you again. So when you leave for New York, don't bother to come back to Vermont because of me."

His rough features hardened in ruthless lines, an icy look in his eyes. "I'm sorry to disappoint you, Bridget, but I'm not going back to New York."

"What?" She stiffened, uncertain what he had meant to imply.

"The reason I was late getting ready for tonight's party is because I'd spent the afternoon in town." Malicious amusement glittered coldly in his eyes at the apprehensive expression on her face. "I had to meet with the real-estate people to sign all the papers for my new home."

"Where?" Bridget drew back and he released her, letting her stand freely in front of him.

"I bought the old Hanson farm. We're neighbors now. Isn't that a pleasant surprise?" he mocked.

She wanted to scream, to pound at the solid wall of his chest, to scratch that complacent expression from his face. But she couldn't. At all costs, she didn't want him to know how destroying his announcement was.

"I'm glad," she lied bravely. "Mr. Hanson had been trying to sell that place for years. Now he'll be able to move into town with his sister. It's a beautiful piece of property, Jonas, I'm sure you'll like it. Congratulations."

He was angered by her calm response. Bridget could see it in the muscle leaping along his jaw. Abruptly he turned away to stride into the kitchen. The victory, temporarily, was Bridget's. She didn't feel like the victor. The sensation was more like that of a survivor.

No one appeared to have noticed that Jonas had left her standing in the middle of a song. Bridget joined the nearest group, letting the cover of their voices and laughter hide her shaky composure. Soon Jim was at her side, handing her the glass of beer he had left to get.

After nearly an hour, what Bridget thought was a decent interval, she suggested to Jim that they leave, pleading a headache. He agreed without hesitation, although his gaze swung to Jonas at the far side of the room, guessing the cause of her headache. Not once did he ask any awkward questions that she would have been reluctant to answer.

TWICE IN THE TWO WEEKS after the party, Bridget saw
Jonas in town, always at a distance. Neither time did
he enter the craft store to see her. She wasn't certain
that he had given up, though, but she had never
pretended she could understand him. A few times
she had believed she did, until that moment ten years
ago, almost eleven years now, when he had told her
he was leaving, ignoring her declarations of love.

Her mother had been incensed when she learned
Jonas was moving back to Vermont, positively livid
when she discovered he had bought the Hanson farm
that abutted their rear property line. Bridget hadn't
told her, but the local grapevine worked rapidly in
her place.

"Mark my words, Bridget, he's up to no good,"
Margaret Harrison had warned her daughter, having
raced over to the chalet the minute she had heard.
"And don't you go getting yourself involved with
him again. I only hope you learned your lesson ten
years ago and have realized what kind of a man he
is."

"Don't worry, mother," Bridget had replied patiently. "It isn't a lesson I'm likely to forget."

Despite Bridget's assurance, Margaret Harrison
seemed to believe it was her duty to remind her
daughter of her warning every time they met. She
was constantly cross-examined as to whether she
had seen or talked to Jonas nearly every day of the
past two weeks. Margaret was invariably skeptical
of Bridget's answers, which did not improve Bridget's already strained disposition.

Bridget was dreading another such interrogation as her parents' large white house came into view around the road's curve. Her own small chalet was hidden briefly by the thick leaves of the trees. Slowing the car, she saw Molly in the garden with her grandfather and honked the horn, relieved that she wouldn't have to go to the house to get Molly.

Glancing up, Molly waved and began sprinting to meet her, tawny chestnut hair tied in pigtails flying behind her. Instead of turning into the driveway of the big house, Bridget turned the car into her own. A breathless Molly reached her as she stepped out of the car.

"You're late," Molly panted. "What happened? I suppose someone came in the shop five minutes before you were going to close."

"I stopped for groceries." Bridget took one of the bags from the backseat. "You can help me carry them in."

"Just what I always wanted to do," Molly grimaced, but obligingly gathered the bag in her arms.

"What did you do today?" Balancing a second sack, Bridget reached for a third.

"Drove grandma up a tree," Molly grinned impishly.

"Oh, Molly!" Bridget couldn't help smiling as she shook her head ruefully. "I suppose you spent the whole day asking her 'What's to do?' "

"Not exactly." Then Molly sighed. "Grandma has just been in a bad mood lately. What's wrong, mom? Why is she so upset?"

Pushing the car door shut with her hip, Bridget tried to avoid the true reason. "Everyone has bad days now and then."

"But she keeps talking about 'that' man lately, saying things like 'why did that man have to come back?' and bugging grandpa if there isn't some way they can make 'that' man go away." Molly frowned, glancing to her mother for an explanation as they climbed the few steps to the chalet's porch.

"Open the door for me, will you?" Bridget requested, stalling for more time while she tried to think of a reply.

Molly shifted the bag of crogeries to one arm and opened the sliding doors. "Today I heard her say to grandpa that she knew 'that' man was going to hurt you again. Who is he, mom? Do you know him?"

"I—" The sentence was never finished. 'That' man was standing in the living-room archway to the kitchen. Anticipating such a meeting for the past two weeks, Bridget recovered quickly from the shock of seeing him to demand stiffly, "What are you doing here, Jonas?"

"I decided it was time to visit my neighbors," he replied calmly. "The door was open, so I walked in." His gaze drifted lazily around him. "This is a nice place you have. I took the liberty of looking around—I hope you don't object."

"It's a little late to object now, isn't it?" she bristled faintly.

"Neighbor?" Molly studied him curiously, not recognizing Jonas as the stranger she had seen briefly several months ago. "Are you the one that bought Mr. Hanson's farm?"

"The same," Jonas inclined his head in mocking acknowledgement, but his gaze flickered coldly to the pigtailed girl standing beside Bridget.

"Put the groceries in the kitchen, Molly. There's one more bag in the car. Would you get it for me?" It was an order, not a suggestion, issued to protect her daughter from the hostility she sensed in Jonas.

"Sure, mom." Molly walked to the kitchen, smiling at Jonas as she went by him, but he didn't return it.

"You'll have to excuse me, Jonas, but I can't stop to have a neighborly chat with you now. I bought some perishables that have to be put away," Bridget explained with false pleasantness and followed her daughter.

"I don't mind waiting until you're through." He deliberately ignored her hint that she wanted him to leave. "Go ahead, I'm in no rush."

Aware of his alert gaze watching her unload the grocery bags through his mask of lazy indifference, Bridget waited until Molly was out of the house before demanding. "Why did you come, Jonas?"

"I wanted to see you," he returned evenly.

"I thought I'd made it plain that I wasn't interested in seeing you." She tried to keep her voice level and aloof as she set the canned goods from the bags onto the counter.

56

Jonas didn't acknowledge the comment. "I couldn't help noticing that there weren't any pictures of your husband around the house."

"I suppose you went through all the rooms!" Bridget flashed.

Again he ignored her remark. "I expected to at least find his photograph by your bedside, but there was only a picture of your daughter in the bedroom."

Her temper simmered near the boiling point. "You don't respect anybody's privacy, do you?"

"Why do you keep avoiding my question, Bridget?" He tipped his head to one side in challenge. "Is there some reason you don't have any photos of your dear, departed husband?" Jonas mocked.

"An excellent one," she snapped. "He didn't like having his picture taken. The only one I have of Brian is a school photo that doesn't resemble him at all. Believe me, if I'd known he was going to be killed so suddenly and you would expect me to produce pictures of him, I would have made certain that some photographs had been taken! Does that answer your question?"

His mouth thinned into a disgruntled line. "It does." Turning away, he raked an impatient hand through the rumpled thickness of his tobacco-brown hair.

At that moment Molly returned with the last bag of groceries. When Bridget noticed the way Jonas was dissecting her daughter with the narrowed sharpness of his gaze, she realized the reason for his question.

It hadn't been because he doubted her husband's existence. He had wanted to know what Brian looked like, possibly curious to see if Bridget had married someone who resembled him. Anger flamed at his arrogant conceit.

"Let me help you, Jonas," she declared hotly. "Molly has Brian's disposition, compassionate and sensitive. In looks, she resembles me, with the exception that she has her father's chin!"

His piercing gaze didn't waver from the little girl, who shifted uncomfortably under his harsh study. Frowning, Molly glanced at Bridget, sensing the violent undercurrents in the atmosphere and feeling confused by them. Bridget's embittered outburst hadn't helped.

Molly looked back at Jonas, frowning darkly. "Who are you?" she demanded with near insolence.

Cold anger hardened his expression. "Why don't you go play with your dolls?" he suggested savagely.

"I'm too old for dolls," Molly declared, arching him a haughty look. "That's kid stuff. Besides, I don't have to go. This is my house."

"She has your stubbornness, too, Bridget," Jonas flashed.

"Molly, I don't think you've fed the horse yet," Bridget inserted pointedly.

"I'll do it after dinner," she shrugged.

"Do it now, Molly," Bridget ordered with forced calm.

The small mouth was pressed tightly closed, rebellion gleaming briefly in Molly's hazel eyes before she stalked to the door leading outside. She yanked it open, then glared over her shoulder.

"He's 'that' man grandma was talking about, isn't he?" she accused and slammed out of the house without waiting for an answer.

"She's only a child, Jonas." Bridget turned back to the grocery sacks. "I don't want her being caught in the middle of our arguments."

"You brought her into it, not me," he reminded her stiffly.

"I am aware of my part in it," she admitted. "But I want you to know that I will not have Molly hurt by what happened between you and me ten—eleven years ago."

"Ten years, four months, and fourteen days ago," he corrected grimly.

"Am I supposed to be impressed that you kept track?" Bridget mocked bitterly.

Frost had accumulated on the frozen orange juice cans in her hands, but the temperature didn't seem any colder than the freezing pain that gripped her chest.

"Will you let those groceries be?" Jonas growled, snatching the cans from her hand and dumping them back in the paper sack. When she would have retrieved them, he caught at her hands to stop her.

"While you're remembering everything so accurately, Jonas, remember also that you were the one to walk out on me," she hurled angrily. "I haven't forgotten that, even if you conveniently have."

"I haven't forgotten. There are a few other things I haven't forgotten, too. Maybe you have."

Before Bridget could make the first attempt to twist her hands free of his grip, Jonas was pulling her into his arms, overpowering her struggling resistance. The familiar pressure of his hard mouth covering hers evoked a storm of memories. Lightning flashed through her veins to kindle the banked fires of passion.

Her lips parted willingly under the expert persuasion of his demanding kiss. Joy thundered in her ears as she once again experienced the wild excitement of his embrace. The frightening explosion of her senses was more awesomely wonderful than she remembered. Every fiber of her being quivered in reaction to the hard, male contour of his body pressed roughly against hers.

She was lost to the emotional upheaval. She was at the mercy of the arousing caress of his hands intimately roaming over her curves. There was satisfaction in feeling him shudder with ultimate longing when he buried his face in the curve of her neck. "Ten years hasn't changed it for either of us," Jonas declared huskily. His hand rested along her throat, his thumb on her pulsing vein. "I can feel your heart racing the same as mine."

Breathing shakily, Bridget slowly pushed herself away from him. Jonas didn't try to stop her, certain now of his power over her. Her fingers raked over her scalp, hesitating for a second at the back of her head in an effort to regain some of her equilibrium.

"I don't deny that you can make me want you, Jonas," she admitted, "but it's strictly chemistry."

"You don't believe that," he shook his head complacently, the flames of desire still smoldering in the gray green depths of his eyes.

"I do," Bridget insisted. "You walked out of my life ten years ago and you aren't going to walk back into it."

"Don't count on it," he warned.

"No, don't you count on it," she returned sharply. "I got along just fine without you and it's going to stay that way. There isn't any room for you in my life. I have Molly and my work and—Jim," she added the last deliberately, knowing that it would anger him.

"You feel safe standing behind him, don't you?" Jonas snapped.

"I'm only stating the way things are," Bridget lied. "You can interpret what I say any way you want to."

"I understand what you're saying." His teeth were clenched tightly against the anger hardening his jaw. "You aren't going to give our relationship a chance to develop into something more."

"I'm giving it the same chance you did, Jonas, when you left—none," she answered coldly. "Please leave my house."

"I don't get any credit for coming back, is that it?" he challenged bleakly.

"Not after ten years, Jonas. You waited too long."

He glared at her for harrowing seconds before he turned on his heel and walked out the door. Not for a minute did Bridget think she had seen the last of him, but she leaned weakly against the counter, grateful for the momentary respite.

How long would it take before his persistence wore her down, she wondered. Already she was beginning to have twinges of doubt. He sounded so sincere. But she had also believed that ten years ago until her mother had revealed his true character.

CHAPTER FOUR

A SOB LODGED ITSELF IN HER THROAT. Jonas had made a fool of her once. Bridget refused to let him do it again. She turned back to the groceries on the counter, trembling as she again began putting them away.

The outer door opened. "He's gone," Molly declared with satisfaction. "I hope you told him off, mom." Her hazel eyes were gleaming with anger. "He is the man grandma was talking about, isn't he?" This time she wanted a definite answer.

"I believe so," Bridget admitted.

"What's his name?"

"Jonas Concannon."

Molly plucked an apple from the sack and bit into it. "I hope grandpa can make him leave."

"You shouldn't say things like that," Bridget reprimanded, but only half-heartedly.

"Why not? It's true. I don't like him. And he doesn't like me."

"You don't know that." But Bridget wasn't certain exactly how Jonas felt toward Molly, except that he resented her. She carried the frozen orange juice to the freezer.

"I can tell," Molly nodded with absolute certainty and peered at the contents of another sack. "Do you like him?"

That was an impossible question to answer. "I don't know. Would you hand me the milk?"

"Did you know him before he came here?" Molly lifted the milk container from the kitchen counter and carried it to Bridget.

"He used to live here."

"When?"

"Before you were born." Bridget wished the questions would end, but Molly rarely left a subject alone until her curiosity was satisfied.

"Did you know him then?"

"Yes, I did."

"Very well?"

If she didn't answer the question, Molly would simply ask someone else, probably her mother. And Bridget didn't want her mother discussing Jonas with Molly.

"I used to go out with him."

"On dates?" Molly made a frowning grimace. "You mean he was your boyfriend?"

"Yes." One sack was empty and Bridget folded it up and put it in a drawer.

"Did you love him?"

Bridget turned sharply. "Don't you think your questions are becoming a little too personal?"

Hearing those words from her daughter struck a raw nerve. For a moment they stared silently at each other, hazel eyes meeting hazel eyes. Molly didn't demand an answer, but her curiosity gleamed brighter than before.

With a sigh, Bridget relented, wishing she had answered it before rather than risk having the importance of her response magnified out of proportion. "I thought I loved him."

"What about my father?"

"There are many kinds of love, Molly," Bridget explained patiently. "You don't love your grandmother in the same way you love me. That's the way it always is. I loved your father very much, or I would never have had you."

Apparently satisfied, Molly chomped another bite from the apple and sauntered to the window overlooking the valley pasture. Bridget released a deep silent sigh of relief and turned to the remaining grocery sacks.

"Still and all," Molly spoke absently, "I wish that man would go away."

"Everything can't always be the way you want it. Jonas has the right to live anywhere he wants to live." Silently Bridget wished that he hadn't chose it to be Vermont, or the Hanson farm.

Molly turned from the window, a perplexed and thoughtful frown on her face, chestnut pigtails trailing down her back. "I heard grandma say that they'd paid him a lot of money to leave once and asked grandpa if they shouldn't do it again. Do you suppose they will?"

Motionless, Bridget tried to find the breath to speak. She would have to have a talk with her mother and remind her of the big ears that children possessed.

"What did your grandfather say to that?" she asked, dodging a direct answer to the question.

Molly nibbled at the corner of her lip, then sighed, "He said he didn't think it would work a second time."

"I think your grandfather is right." She was voicing her first opinion, but had to concede it was possible Jonas had returned for that very reason. "Did you dust the furniture today?"

"Yes. Can I go into town with you tomorrow to see Vicki?" Molly tossed the apple core into the waste basket.

"We'll see."

"Please," she coaxed. "It's boring all by myself all day."

"You aren't by yourself, Molly. You have—"

"Grandpa and grandma don't count," she declared with a disgruntled groan.

"Maybe you can come in tomorrow afternoon," Bridget smiled.

"Great!" The frown disappeared in a burst of exuberance. "When do we eat?"

"As soon as I have the rest of these groceries put away. In the meantime, why don't you wash your hands and start fixing a salad?"

"Okay," Molly agreed readily and moved toward

the hallway to the bathroom. She paused at the hall
entrance, her hand resting against the wall. Glancing
over her shoulder, she said to Bridget, "Imagine his
thinking that *I* still played with dolls!" an adult-like
expression of cutting disdain on her youthful face.

"Imagine," Bridget murmured dryly to herself as
her daughter disappeared.

BRIDGET WAS FORCED to postpone the discussion
with her mother until the weekend. The evenings
when she was home Molly was naturally nearby, and
since the object of the discussion was to warn her
mother not to talk about Jonas when Molly was
around, Bridget would have been disregarding her
own advice. She waited until Molly had saddled her
Morgan mare, a daughter of the mare Mr. Harrison
owned, and gone for a ride. Then she walked across
the road to the big house.

As usual the house was immaculate, a reflection of
its fastidious mistress. The woodwork and furniture
were polished to a glowing sheen. Not a speck of dust
lurked anywhere. Sunlight gleamed through clean
windows accenting the pristine whiteness of the
curtains.

Brightly colored throw pillows were plumped and
artfully arranged on the plush sofa, seeming to deny
that an elbow had ever rested against them. Books
were orderly and arranged on the shelves with not a
single magazine or newspaper on any of the tables.
Bridget always had the impression she was looking

at a room about to be photographed for a magazine, régardless of which room of the house she was in.

Her mother's initial delight at Bridget's unexpected visit didn't last long. She had launched immediately into what she presumed was the correct mother-older-daughter chatter until Bridget interrupted to explain the reason for her visit. Margaret Harrison's indignation was immediate, she was affronted that she should be reprimanded by her daughter.

"Your father and I were talking privately. I had no idea at all that Molly was listening," she defended. "I certainly wouldn't even have mentioned the man if I had."

"I know that, mother," Bridget replied patiently. "I'm merely suggesting that if you must mention Jonas, don't do it when Molly is around. She's at an impressionable age. She's already read between the lines of what she overheard and has formed a prejudice against Jonas."

"You certainly don't expect me to encourage her to like him, do you?" Her mother stiffened visibly. "After the way he treated you, I would think you would want to make certain Molly had nothing to do with him."

"You misunderstand my reason. I don't see any reason for Molly to know about what happened ten years ago. Thanks to you, she does have a general idea, and that's where I want it to end. That's why I want you to be cautious when you speak of Jonas around Molly." Bridget lifted the delicate china cup from its saucer and inhaled the aroma of freshly brewed tea, hot and strong the way she liked it.

"Personally I think it's a good idea that Molly should be warned what kind of a man he is," her mother sniffed, her dark head regally erect, not a brunette hair out of place. "If he has returned to Randolph with the thought of winning you back, as I strongly believe he has, then I'm certain he wouldn't be above stooping to use Molly to get you. I'm positive he'll try to win her affections. What better way of getting to you and persuading you to forgive him?"

It was a very plausible theory and it might have eroded Bridget's resolve not to be taken in by Jonas again. Except it had a weak point.

"I think you're wrong, mother," she insisted.

"I doubt it. The man is completely unscrupulous. He would do anything and use anyone to get what he wanted. He's proved that as far as I'm concerned. You above all should agree with me," was the emphatic response.

"I know what you mean, but . . . ." Bridget hesitated, trying to put into words something she only sensed. "Jonas resents Molly, I think, as Brian's child. It was obvious the other day when—" Bridget stopped. She hadn't meant to tell her mother of Jonas's visit.

"—When he told Molly to go play with her dolls," her mother said with a faint air of superiority, as if nothing could be hidden from her for long. At Bridget's startled glance, she smiled complacently. "Molly told me all about it. Or have you seen him since then?"

"No, I haven't," resenting the way her mother could make her feel guilty as if she was still a child.

"It's a shame when my own granddaughter has to tell me things that my daughter should have."

"I didn't see that there was anything to tell," Bridget defended her silence about the meeting. "I asked Jonas to leave and he did."

"The next time he comes over, I wouldn't even open the door to him if I were you."

Obviously Molly hadn't told her grandmother that Jonas had been waiting inside the house for them. Bridget didn't bother to enlighten her. She sipped at her tea, making no comment at all.

"I saw him in town the other day," Margaret Harrison spoke absently. "Of course, he didn't see me," she hastened. "But I noticed the way the women seemed to gravitate to him, staring at him whether he looked their way or not. Tell me the truth, Bridget. Are you still attracted to him?"

"You know the old saying, mother, 'once bitten, twice shy.'" But she was attracted to him. All the wariness in the world didn't alter that. Bridget replaced her cup in its saucer and straightened from the wing-backed chair. "I have a lot to do. I'd better be getting back to the house."

"Must you?" her mother sighed ruefully.

"Yes," Bridget insisted.

"You and Molly come over for dinner this evening, then."

Bridget opened her mouth to refuse, then shrugged, "What time?"

"Is six too early?"

"That's fine. See you later." She walked quickly to the front door before her mother could succeed in delaying her a few more minutes.

Outside, Bridget paused on the gray porch steps of the house, struck for an instant by the vivid hues of green painting the valley and the rolling hills. The green of the land brilliantly contrasted with the blue of the sky, the air startlingly clear and fresh with scents of summer.

Her gaze made an admiring sweep of the verdant scenery. It was a rejuvenating view that lightened her footsteps. She spied her father near the barn working on the farm tractor and smiled at the sight of him in denim coveralls, his hands covered with grease and a straw hat on top of his head.

Despite all the money he had made selling vast acreage of his land for real-estate development, he was still a farmer at heart. Earthy, easygoing, he was the complete opposite of his wife and was the steady anchor that had kept Margaret Harrison from becoming too puffed up with an inflated sense of her own importance.

"Hi, dad!" Bridget waved.

He glanced up, surprised, wiping his hands on a

snowy white kerchief. Bridget could hear her mother wailing when she saw it. "Well, hello, princess," he smiled and looked to the house. "I didn't realize you'd stopped by. Molly was just here looking for you."

"Did she say what she wanted?" She frowned curiously.

"No, I—there she is now." His gaze had made a searching swing, sighting his granddaughter on the other side of the road. "Just coming around the chalet."

Bridget saw Molly astride the bay horse at almost the same instant that Molly saw her and waved. "I'll go see what she wants. See you later, dad."

Molly met her at the mailbox by the road. "I didn't know where you were."

"I went over to have a cup of tea with your grandmother." Bridget made light of her visit. "Dad said you were looking for me."

"Yes, I want you to come riding with me." She leaned forward in the saddle. "Please, mom. I don't feel like riding alone."

"I'd like to, honey, but I have a lot of housework to do," she said, a touch of regret in her smile.

"You haven't gone riding with me for over two weeks," Molly argued. Bridget knew it was true. She hadn't been riding since she learned that Jonas had purchased the adjoining farm. "Please come with me and I'll help with the housework when we get back—I promise."

"Well—" Bridget hesitated and Molly knew she had won.

"You go change into your boots and I'll saddle Flash." She didn't wait for Bridget to agree as she reined the small bay around to ride to the horse shed behind the chalet.

Bridget glanced at the cloudless blue sky and the inviting green of the hills and shrugged. It was too beautiful a day for housework.

It took only a few minutes to change out of her sandals into a pair of boots and to tie the sleeves of a sweater around her neck in case it was cool riding. But the usually difficult-to-catch sorrel mare was tied to the fence, saddled and bridled, swishing her flaxen tail at the flies. Molly giggled at the look of surprise on Bridget's face.

"I had her all ready just in case you decided to come," she explained mischievously.

"Just don't you forget you promised to help with the housework," Bridget laughed and untied the reins from the post and swung aboard the horse. "You lead the way. Flash and I will follow."

"We'll play follow the leader," Molly called over her shoulder and guided the bay through the gate.

At a canter, they wound through the green pasture dotted with wild flowers and splashed through a small stream to enter the sugar bush of maple trees. A solid canopy of leaves was overhead as Molly set a twisting course through the trees, dodging branches that threatened to decapitate the unwary.

At the end of the sugar bush, a crumbling stone wall stood in their way. Bridget started to slow the sorrel, but Molly didn't check her mount, setting the bay at the low wall. Gracefully the Morgan soared over the obstacle with easily a foot to spare. There was a lump of pride in Bridget's throat at the degree of horsemanship displayed by her daughter. She too urged her mount to the wall and jumped it cleanly.

Molly had reined in on the other side to wait, the bay mare snorting and blowing, still fresh to go many a mile more, but docilely waiting for the command. Bridget saw the breathless exhilaration on Molly's face and guessed that her own expression matched it.

"Are you glad you came?" Molly grinned.

"What do you think, you little minx?" Bridget laughed, reining in the sorrel next to her daughter. "How long have you been jumping Satin?"

"Grandpa and I have been schooling her since early spring. I wanted to surprise you, though," Molly beamed.

"You certainly accomplished that!" It had all happened too quickly for Bridget to feel more than brief alarm.

"Grandpa says she's a natural jumper, but then Satin can do anything." Molly stroked the mare's neck.

"Almost anything," Bridget cautioned.

"Almost," Molly conceded, wrinkling her nose in impish qualification. "I might start showing her next summer. Of course, we'll need a horse trailer."

"A minor, inexpensive item," Bridget teased.

"Can we afford it?" suddenly serious.

"Oh, we might be able to buy a couple of wheels and a crate. We'll see," she mocked.

"Honestly, mom. Grandpa said—"

"You didn't mention this to your grandfather, did you, Molly?" Bridget sighed. She preferred to manage on her own without running to her parents for loans.

"Yes, when I was talking about showing Satin," Molly admitted. "He said he might be able to find a used one that we could fix up."

"You mean that your grandfather would fix up." Bridget nudged the sorrel into a walk, trying to estimate how much a used horse van might cost and how much she could risk spending out of her savings.

"We really should buy it this summer so it could be all ready to go next year," Molly offered hesitantly.

"We'll have to see how much they cost first. I haven't any idea."

"Shall I have grandpa start looking for one?" Molly eyed her mother hopefully.

"I'll talk to him about it," Bridget promised.

"When?"

"We're going to have dinner with them tonight. Is that soon enough?" Her laughing hazel eyes gleamed brightly at the widened look of delight rounding Molly's eyes.

"It sure is," Molly breathed.

As they trotted their horses through a small stand of trees, sunlight streamed through the branches to dapple the ground. Last year's autumn leaves made a pleasant rustling sound beneath the horse's hooves. Overhead a jay called raucously, flitting from limb to limb to follow them.

"He sure didn't waste any time," Molly muttered.

"What?" Bridget glanced blankly at her daughter.

"Putting up new signs to post his property." Molly gestured to a new white signboard nailed to a tree near the fence line. No Hunting and No Trespassing, the sign read. "As if anyone would hurt his precious property," she added sarcastically.

Bridget paled; realizing that they were riding through Jonas's land. Boundary lines had never been observed in the past. They had always ridden this way since she was a young girl. The only difference this time had been that they had jumped the stone wall instead of using the gate.

Mr. Hanson had posted No Trespassing signs, but he hadn't meant them for his neighbor. Bridget doubted if Jonas did, but the circumstances weren't the same.

"Crackers! There he is!" Molly exclaimed in a low hiss. "Come on, mom. Let's go before he catches up to us."

Bridget barely had time to lift her gaze to the hill rising on their right and identify Jonas sitting tall on a rangy bay horse before Molly was digging her heels into her horse. The eager mare bounded forward.

76

"Molly!" Bridget tried to call her back, for an instant checking the attempt of her own mount to follow.

She was more anxious than her daughter to avoid meeting Jonas, but it was foolish to run, foolish and juvenile. Yet Molly was juvenile and Bridget could hardly let her go running headlong over the rolling terrain alone.

With the relaxing of the pressure holding it back, her sorrel Flash needed no second urging to race after its stable companion. The thunder of hooves pounding the grassy sod drowned out all other sounds.

There was no time to look back to see if Jonas was following. At this pace, Bridget had to focus her attention on what lay ahead. It was certain he had seen them, and she could guess his amusement at their flight.

A hundred yards from their starting point, a white board fence, the wood chipped and graying, blocked their access to the public graveled road. As they neared it, Bridget turned her horse toward the gate only a few yards farther up from the point of approach, slowing the sorrel. But Molly didn't alter her course, only checking her mount to set it for the jump.

"No!" Bridget shouted. "Molly, no!"

It was too late. The horse and rider were already arching over the fence. They landed cleanly on the other side, only to have a road ditch yawn before

77

them. Bridget heard the motor of an approaching vehicle and yelled a panicked warning.

She didn't think Molly had heard her. Either way it didn't matter because the mare's impetus would carry them into the road, the Morgan gallantly collecting itself to leap the ditch.

The horse landed on the graveled shoulder at the same instant that the pickup truck topped the small knoll. Bridget saw Molly sawing frantically on the reins to stop the horse and the driver swerving to the opposite ditch to avoid hitting them.

The Morgan attempted a sharp turn, lost its footing in the loose gravel and fell. Bridget heard her daughter's cry of fear as she was thrown from the saddle and someone screaming Molly's name over and over, unaware the scream came from her own throat.

Driven by the desperate need to reach her daughter, Bridget abandoned caution, jumping the sorrel over the fence gate where an earth-covered culvert eliminated the open-drainage ditch. Molly lay motionless along the side of the ditch as Bridget rode up, dismounting almost before the sorrel had stopped.

The battered pickup had stopped several yards down the road. The driver, gaunt and aging, came huffing up the small incline, his fear showing in the graying color beneath his suntan.

"I'm sorry, she just came out of nowhere. I couldn't stop," he explained in a thin voice as

Bridget knelt beside her daughter. "Is she badly hurt?"

"I don't know." Her voice throbbed with fear. She reached for the unconscious girl. "Molly?"

"Don't move her!" a familiar voice barked a second before a pair of rough hands pushed Bridget out of the way.

Bridget was too shaken by the sight of Molly's white face to protest as Jonas assumed control. Dazed, she didn't question his right. Her hands were clasped tightly together in a silent prayer that Molly was not seriously hurt.

"Is there something I can do?" The elderly man hovered above them, watching anxiously as Jonas ran exploring hands over Molly's inert form. "Shall I call an ambulance? There's a house just up the road and—"

"It's my house," Jonas informed him curtly, not letting his gaze stray from Molly. "And I don't think we'll need an ambulance."

"She can be moved, then," Bridget breathed, her lashes fluttering downward in relief that Jonas believed there was no risk of a crippling injury.

"I wish there was something I could do," the older man mumbled to himself.

Gray green eyes made a sharp, assessing sweep of the older man, noting the man's shock and advanced age. The hard line of his mouth curved briefly into an understanding smile.

"We'd be grateful if you'd drive us to the house,"

79

Jonas told him, but there was nothing understanding in the look he darted at Bridget. "Catch the horses and get them off the road."

"Leave Molly?" she gasped in angered astonishment.

"We don't need another accident," he snapped and returned his attention to Molly, closing the discussion.

Although Bridget recognized the wisdom and logic behind his order, his lack of compassion was a flame to her temper. She wanted to disobey even as she rose shakily to her feet to comply, her knees weak and her stomach churning.

The rangy bay Jonas had been riding stood ground hitched behind them. Bridget grabbed at the reins and walked across the road to where her sorrel was grazing along the graveled shoulder.

The recalcitrant horse, for once, allowed Bridget to walk right up to her as if knowing this was not the time to play a game of tag. Molly's bay mare was standing by the board fence, a knee scraped and bloody but showing no other marks from the fall.

Leading the three horses, Bridget started back to Molly. She stopped short at the sight of her daughter gently and carefully cradled in Jonas's arms and Jonas climbing into the pickup.

"I'll meet you at the house," he ordered, indifferent to her frown of shocked anger. "Put the horses in the pen behind the barn."

How dare he take Molly and leave her! Bridget

flared as the pickup door closed and the truck began rattling up the road. She should be the one with Molly and he should be bringing the horses. But it was too late to argue the point.

Bridget quickly mounted her sorrel mare and tugged the other horses into a trot. His house was only a quarter of a mile up the road. At that moment, she hated Jonas as passionately as she had once loved him.

The pickup truck traveled slowly and she was able to stay close, taking a short cut across the open lawn to the rear of the house and the barns. As she dismounted to open the gate of the pen, she glimpsed Jonas carrying Molly into the house. Her daughter was still limp and unconscious in his arms. Quickly Bridget chased the horses into the pen, closed the gate, and ran toward the house.

CHAPTER FIVE

BRIDGET STORMED INTO THE HOUSE, slammed the screen door and followed the sound of Jonas's voice to the room where he had gone.

"I saw the whole thing, Mr. Johnson. It was a damned fool stunt to jump that fence to the road. You weren't in any way to blame for what happened," he was saying to assure the elderly driver. "In fact, it's a miracle you were able to avoid hitting her."

When Bridget entered the living room, Molly was lying inertly on the couch. Jonas sat on the edge near her and the gaunt, elderly man stood beside them, his features still strained.

"I tell you when I saw her and that horse on the road, it liked to scare ten years off my life, and I ain't got ten years to spare," the man shook his head. "You sure she's going to be all right?"

"Nothing seems to be broken. She'll be scraped and bruised, but she'll be coming to shortly." Jonas glanced up as Bridget hurried to the couch. "Mrs. O'Shea and I thank you for stopping and giving us a ride."

His comment was a pointed reminder that she hadn't expressed her gratitude. Bridget hesitated beside the couch, irritated by his subtle criticism.

"Yes, thank you, Mr.—Johnson," she offered tightly.

"It's okay." He waved aside her thanks. "If you're sure everything's all right and you won't be needing me anymore, I'd better be getting home. The missus will be wondering where I am."

"You take it easy, Mr. Johnson," Jonas said in goodbye.

"Don't worry, I will," the man said, leaving the room.

"It's damned lucky he didn't have a heart attack," Jonas muttered beneath his breath, straightening from the couch as the back door to the house opened and closed.

Bridget moved away from the couch, walking swiftly to the black telephone she noticed on a table near an armchair. "I'll call the hospital to notify the emergency room that we're bringing Molly in."

"There's no need," Jonas retorted.

"No need!" Bridget pivoted angrily to confront him. "You seem determined to overlook the fact that Molly is my daughter! First you order me not to touch her, then you push me out of the way so I can't even see how she is. Then you cart her off and tell me to bring the horses."

"Be sensible, Bridget," he said with tight-lipped patience. "You were in no state to determine rationally how severe her injuries were. The horses had to be got off the road and Johnson was in no condition to chase them. And as for taking your daughter and leaving you, I don't think you're strong enough to carry an eighty-pound child, nor was Johnson. That left me. Regarding the hospital, I'm merely advising you that I don't believe it's necessary."

"I don't have to listen to your advice!" she flared. His reasonable explanation for his actions only increased her agitation. She was too concerned about Molly to care about logic. "None of this would have happened if it hadn't been for you! It's all you fault! Molly was running from you! She would never have jumped that fence if it hadn't been for you! You're to blame—you and—"

The flat of his hand struck her cheek in a stinging slap. Bridget's arm swung to retaliate in kind, hot tears burning her eyes, but his fingers caught her wrist, stopping her attempt.

"You were becoming hysterical," Jonas informed her coldly. "It was either slap you or kiss you, and my mood is a little too violent for the latter."

Abruptly he released her arm and turned away. Some of her anger had dissipated at his chilling rebuke, but not all of it.

"Where are you going?" she demanded.

Jonas halted, his rugged features drawn forbiddingly grim, a frosty glint in his eyes. "To get a cold compress for that bump on her head, some antiseptic to clean the cuts and abrasions and some ammonia to bring her around."

"Don't bother!" she snapped. "You aren't going

to lay a hand on her. I'm taking Molly to the hospital whether you think it's necessary or not!"

"For God's sake, Bridget!" Jonas exclaimed in a savagely low voice. "I know you think I'm untrustworthy as hell as a man, but you could at least credit me with some degree of competency in my work!"

Her chin lifted, wary and confused. "Your work?"

"Don't pretend ignorance," he jeered with contempt. "You know damned well I'm a doctor."

Stunned, she opened her mouth, her voice temporarily deserting her. "I—I didn't—know," she finally stammered out.

"Come on," Jonas laughed his disbelief, harsh and biting. "Everyone knows it. Bob, Evelyn, everyone."

"I didn't, Jonas, I swear," Bridget murmured. At the skepticism still freezing his gaze, she hastened an explanation. "I've never talked about you or asked about you. No one volunteered it. I imagine for the same reason you didn't know about Brian."

He breathed in deeply, an eyebrow lifting in a frown as if he was testing the comparison. He seemed about to comment when Molly moaned softly and he turned away. This time Bridget didn't accuse him of trying to usurp her position when he sat on the edge of the couch beside Molly.

"Mom?" she called in a questioning groan, her eyes opening slowly.

"I'm right here, honey," Bridget assured her, kneeling next to the arm of the couch.

85

"How do you feel, Molly? Jonas inquired calmly, a professional mask stealing over the features that a moment ago had been hardened in anger.

"I don't know," she frowned. "I hurt."

She started to lift a hand to the bump on her forehead, but Jonas checked the attempt. "You banged your head," he told her. "That was a foolish thing you did."

A scowl of dislike replaced the slightly dazed frown. "I wanted to get away from you," Molly answered.

"You nearly accomplished that in a very permanent fashion," Jonas nodded. "You're lucky that truck didn't hit you."

"Satin?" Molly breathed in alarm.

"She's fine," Bridget smiled, a fine mist of tears brightening her hazel eyes. "Like you, she has a few cuts and probably some bruises."

"I want to see her." Molly tried to sit up, but Jonas pushed her back.

"Not yet. First we have to get you cleaned up, then you can worry about your horse." Standing, he glanced at Bridget. "Stay here. I'll be right back."

It was an unnecessary order. Bridget had no intention of leaving Molly's side. She moved closer, her smile slightly weak and tremulous.

"Are you sure you're all right, honey?" she murmured.

"I think so." Molly began to shake a little. "I was so scared, mom."

"So was I," Bridget laughed softly. "Whatever made you do that?"

"I don't know," Molly shivered. "I just didn't think about there being any traffic."

Jonas returned and Bridget shifted to the side. "The blouse is pretty well ruined. I'm going to cut the sleeve away. Is that all right?" He glanced briefly at Bridget.

"Of course."

"What's he going to do?" Molly eyed him warily.

"I'm going to clean those scrapes on your arm and leg. You have gravel and dirt in them," answered Jonas.

"I don't want you to do it." Molly drew back against the sofa, mutiny darkening her eyes as she glared at him with dislike.

"He's a doctor, Molly," Bridget offered, hoping to placate her daughter.

"I don't care. I don't want him to touch me," Molly declared.

"She does take after you in that, doesn't she, Bridget?" Jonas muttered cynically.

Bridget flushed. The resentment glittering in her eyes echoed that in her daughter's, but Jonas didn't glance her way to see it.

"You don't have any choice in the matter, Molly," he continued, "because I'm going to clean them." He took hold of the torn sleeve of her blouse and began snipping away to expose the scraped flesh on her arm. Molly tried to twist away. "And you'd better hold still. These scissors are sharp and you could end up with a nasty cut," he warned.

"You're a bully," Molly accused sullenly.

"So I've been told," Jonas responded dryly and began cleaning the abrasion that ran almost the length of her arm.

At the touch of the antiseptic against her skin, Molly flinched and Bridget winced sympathetically, knowing it had to burn.

"That hurts," Molly protested.

A corner of his mouth quirked upward without humor, his gaze not straying from his task. "Did you think it would tickle?"

"You're not much of a doctor," Molly said, clenching her teeth.

"You aren't much of a rider," Jonas retorted.

"I am, too."

"On that flea bitten nag?" he scoffed.

"Satin is not a nag!" Molly defended with outrage. "She is a registered Morgan and a lot better horse than yours, whatever it is."

"What do you know about Morgan horses?" He flashed the little girl a mocking look.

Bridget bridled at the way he was deliberately baiting Molly. She was no match for his sharp tongue. It wasn't fair of him to pick on the child and antagonize her further.

"A lot," Molly declared. "Justin Morgan lived right here in Randolph—the man, not the horse."

"Where did the horse live?"

"The horse lived here, too, but his name wasn't Justin Morgan."

"You just said it was," Jonas mocked.

"No, the man's name was Justin Morgan and the horse was called Figure. Later on, when he got to be famous, they started to call him Morgan's horse," Molly explained sharply, despite his attempt to confuse her.

"Why was he famous? What made him so special?"

"Jonas, what are you trying to prove?" Bridget interrupted angrily, unable to remain silent any longer.

"Stay out of it," he ordered smoothly. "This discussion is between Molly and myself. Unless she doesn't know the answer to my question." The last challenging remark was directed to Molly.

"Of course I know." She snapped up the invisible glove immediately. "The Morgan horse was special because he could do everything. He could work in the woods all day hauling logs, sometimes pulling logs that other, bigger draft horses couldn't and he could run faster than anything around."

"He probably was a bad-tempered brute," Jonas observed.

"He was as gentle as a kitten. And he was the first American breed of horse," Molly declared.

"I guess that's something," Jonas acknowledged with a mild little shrug and shifted his attention to her leg, cutting a slit up the pants leg.

"That isn't all." Molly sat up slightly. Now that she was beginning to impress him with her knowledge, she wanted to enlarge on it. "The other American breeds like the American saddle horse, the Standardbred and the Tennesse walking horse—all of them can be traced back to show a Morgan cross in their beginnings."

"And you think your horse is as special, do you?"

"Satin can do anything," Molly defended stoutly.

"Jonas, will you quit picking on her?" Bridget demanded in a low voice and received an indifferent look for an answer.

"If your horse is as smart as you say it is, it wouldn't have jumped the fence into the road without first checking to see if there was any traffic approaching," he pointed out.

"Satin didn't notice the road," Molly offered lamely, scowling at the fault he had found with her treasured mare.

"She should have looked where she was going," Jonas suggested dryly.

"Yes, but she was really super clearing the fence, then managing to leap the ditch almost right after," she enthused.

"Right in front of a truck," he commented with an absent frown. "Your knee is going to have to be bandaged. You have a fairly deep gash there. I'll get some gauze and adhesive and be right back."

As he straightened from the couch, Bridget hesitated only a second. Touching Molly's hand lightly, she said, "Lie still," and followed Jonas into an adjoining room.

Jonas barely glanced at her as he opened a metal cabinet. His aloofness was another irritant to her already fraying temper, the fire of it sparkling in her eyes. With hands on her hips, she thrust her chin forward to a challenging angle.

"What did you think you were doing in there, baiting Molly that way?" Bridget kept her voice low so Molly couldn't overhear, but it was no less angry because it lacked volume.

Jonas smiled coolly, without amusement. "You don't care for my 'bedside manner?'"

"I found it appalling," she hissed. "I know you don't like Molly, but did you have to make it so obvious? She's a sensitive child and I won't have you ridiculing her. Isn't it enough that she was hurt because she was running from you? Or are you using her to get back at me because I don't want to become involved with you again?"

"My methods may be questionable, Bridget," he replied in a level voice, "but they had the desired results. Your daughter doesn't show the signs of a concussion, her abrasions have been treated and the cut is about to be bandaged—" he raised his hand to indicate the adhesive tape and gauze he held "—without any temper tantrums over whether I was going to take care of her or not. If you want to read something more into my behavior, that's your affair."

He walked briskly past Bridget to return to the living room of the old farmhouse, leaving her to wonder if she had been overimaginative. One thing was clear: Jonas hadn't denied that he resented Molly. Sighing, Bridget felt trapped as she walked back to join them.

"How does the head feel?" Jonas asked, applying the last strip of adhesive.

"How do you think it feels? It tickles," Molly retorted with a sarcasm Bridget hadn't know her daughter possessed.

The grooves deepened near his mouth although he didn't smile. "It will tickle a lot more. Do you want to try to walk to the car and I'll drive you and your mother home?"

Molly nodded gamely, wincing as she accepted his assistance off the couch. She was decidedly unsteady on her feet, a stiffness having already set in to add its discomfort to her bruised body.

Fiercely independent, she shrugged away Bridget's attempt to help her as if she had something to prove to Jonas. Watching Molly closely, his compelling, male features wearing an expression of clinical indifference, he followed them to his station wagon parked in front of the garage.

Gritting her teeth, Molly made it all the way. Bridget heard the painful sigh of relief her daughter made when she relaxed against her in the front seat. Jonas made no comment as he slid behind the wheel and started the car.

There was only silence as they began the drive back until they reached the Y in the road. A left turn would take them to the chalet and a right would lead them to town. Jonas slowed the station wagon nearly to a stop.

He glanced at Bridget. "Would you like me to take you in so your own doctor can examine her?"

To spite him, she nearly said yes. But the fact that he had relented slightly and her own faith that Jonas's opinion regarding Molly was right made her answer truthfully.

"As you said, I don't think it's necessary," she murmured.

"I offered." Jonas shrugged and took the left fork in the road.

In the driveway of the chalet he walked around to the passenger side as Bridget helped Molly slide out of the car. Getting out was proving more painful than getting in, as her stiff and sore body was not co-ordinating properly.

Impatiently Jonas shouldered Bridget aside. "I'll carry her in."

"No!" Molly cried in protest, but she was swept into his arms before she could do anything to stop him.

Bridget knew it was just as much rigid dislike as soreness that made Molly hold herself so stiffly. Jonas could have been carrying a mannequin for all the attention he paid to Molly.

They hadn't reached the chalet steps when her

mother's voice halted them. "Bridget!" My God, what happened? What's wrong with Molly?"

Turning, Bridget saw Margaret Harrison rushing across the road, running while still maintaining a ladylike air. Glancing at Molly, she realized her daughter looked a mess.

There was a goose-egg-size lump on her forehead and a red graze on her cheek. The checked blouse was dirty, the cut sleeve hanging loosely to reveal the long, angry-looking abrasion. Her jeans were cut away from her leg, the white bandage around the knee showing plainly against the blue. Indeed she looked much more seriously hurt than she was.

"Ah, here comes mother," Jonas murmured sarcastically beneath his breath, his lips barely moving. "Living right across the road, she can keep a close eye on you. Tell me, Bridget, does she still vet all your boyfriends to see if they're suitable for you?"

"My mother may be overly possessive and nosy," she bristled, "but her ability to judge the true character of people is faultless."

"You really believe that, don't you?" Although his mouth was twisted in sardonic humor, cold fires of anger blazed in his gray green eyes.

"Yes." Bridget was unable to expand further on her reply as her mother came into their hearing.

"Molly, baby, what happened?" Margaret Harrison demanded in alarm when she saw her granddaughter's tattered state.

"She had a rather nasty fall from her horse,"

Jonas answered. "She has a few cuts, some abrasions and probably a lot of bruises, but no serious injuries."

"You look terrible, Molly," she breathed—hardly a remark that would make the little girl feel better. "Will she be scarred?"

"No, Mrs. Harrison," Jonas answered with veiled disgust. "They'll all fade in time." He slid a piercing look at Bridget. "If you'll open the door, I'll take your daughter inside."

Quickly Bridget stepped forward to open the door and hold it for him. When she would have followed him inside, her mother caught at her arm.

Whispering, Margaret Harrison accused, "You didn't let him treat Molly, did you?"

"He is a doctor," Bridget defended her decision.

"Yes, I know—" her mother began.

"You could have told me he was," Bridget attacked briefly. "It might have saved me some embarrassment."

"I presumed you knew," was the insistently innocent response.

"It doesn't matter," Bridget declared, shaking her head in faint exasperation. Her previous ignorance had already done its damage. Turning, she walked into the house with her mother following.

Margaret Harrison glanced around the empty living room. "Where has he taken her?"

"I imagine to her bedroom," Bridget replied stiffly.

"But how would he know where it is?"

"I would guess Molly told him, wouldn't you?" she retorted and kept silent about his previous exploration of the house when no one was home.

Jonas had to have noticed Molly's bedroom in the loft. It couldn't have been mistaken for hers, not when the walls were a patchwork of posters of whoever happened to be Molly's idol at the moment.

"Yes, of course you're right." Her mother agreed with the plausible explanation.

Bridget started toward the open stairwell leading to the solitary room in the loft. At that moment Jonas appeared at the top of the steps, hesitating for a fraction of a second as he looked at her before descending.

"She's changing into some clean clothes," he stated.

"She'll need some help. I'll go up," Margaret Harrison declared, hurrying quickly up the steps Jonas had just come down.

Jonas watched her disappear, then turned. "It's a pity your mother's marriage can't offer her more fulfilment. Maybe then she wouldn't have to find it living through you," he commented cynically. "Either that or your father should have given her a whole brood of children so she wouldn't have time to meddle in your life."

Bridget stiffened, slightly indignant that he should voice his opinion, however accurate it might be, about something that was none of his business. As far as she was concerned when he walked away ten years ago, he had forfeited any chance of making her personal and family life any of his business.

"Children aren't always the answer." She started to walk past him to the stairs.

"Molly's head might begin to ache." His tone was cool and professional. "If it does, give her a couple of aspirins. If that doesn't relieve it, call me. Or you can contact your own doctor."

"Very well," not saying whom she would call, although she knew Jonas was closer if she needed him. Again she started up the steps.

"I'll bring the horses over later this afternoon," he told her curtly.

With one foot on the stairs, Bridget paused. "I haven't thanked you for all—" Grudgingly she began to express her appreciation, but as she turned, she discovered she was talking to no one but herself.

The front door was closing behind Jonas. She trembled weakly. He seemed to have taken some of her strength with him when he left.

CHAPTER SIX

AFTER DINNER, near sundown, Bridget looked out the kitchen window and noticed the light shining in the window of the horse shed. She guessed that it had to be Jonas returning the horses. She hesitated at the sink, then quickly wiped her hands on a dish towel.

There was the tack to be cleaned and put away and the horses to be fed. She couldn't let Jonas do that. She was already in his debt because of Molly. And that was another thing she wanted to clear up.

Glancing over the breakfast bar into the living room, Bridget could see Molly lying on the sofa in front of the television. She was wearing a loose-fitting cotton robe of Bridget's to keep from irritating the abrasions on her arm and leg.

"Molly, Jonas has brought the horses back. I'm going out to take care of them," she called to her daughter, but didn't receive an answer. She walked part way into the living room and saw that Molly had fallen asleep.

Bridget debated whether or not to waken her, then decided against it. She would probably be back in the house before Molly woke to find her gone. Quietly she slipped out the back door of the house and hurried to the stables. The golden shadows of sunset were coloring the green hills rising from the valley meadow.

Unlatching the door, she swung it open and stepped inside. A breathy excitement gripped her lungs, a sensation she always experienced on meeting Jonas. She was greeted by the pungent odor of horse liniment burning her nose and the nicker of a horse.

The sorrel mare, Flash, was in her stall, the well-formed head turned, ears pricked at Bridget's entrance. But it was the adjoining stall where the gleaming hindquarters of Molly's bay were visible that drew Bridget's gaze. She could hear the rustle of straw and the low, soft crooning of a masculine voice.

Bridget walked to the end of the stall and stopped as Jonas straightened from his crouch beside the bay's front legs. In the shadowy glow of the overhead light bulb, his hair was rumpled and gold lights glistening in the brown thickness.

He was tall and lean and ruggedly primitive, the way she remembered him, with a faded denim jacket hanging open, a worn cotton shirt opened at the throat and snug-fitting Levi's that molded the muscular length of his thighs and legs.

There was a veiled intensity in the way his eyes returned her look. Temporarily Bridget forgot why she had come to the shed, her voice forgetting how to work.

"How's Molly?" Jonas turned slightly, picking up the bottle of liniment from the manger to cap it.

"Fine," she nodded jerkily.

"I fed and watered the horses, cleaned the tack and put it away." He ran a stroking hand over the bay's flank, pushing the horse aside to walk from the stall.

"There was no need for you to do that," Bridget protested. Her poise returned along with common sense that warned her not to let his sensual attraction take possession of her faculties. "I didn't expect it."

His gaze briefly swept her figure, an unnervingly thorough study despite its swiftness. "It was no trouble," he shrugged indifferently and walked by her to replace the liniment in the metal cabinet on the far wall.

"Perhaps not, but I—"

Jonas interrupted as if he didn't care what else she had to say. "The mare's right fetlock is slightly swollen. You might have your father look at it or call a vet."

"I—I'll do that," Bridget replied, momentarily nonplussed.

"I'd like to see Molly before I leave," he stated.

"She's fine," she assured him quickly, not wanting to invite him into the house.

A mocking light entered his eyes, his mouth quirked slightly. "Do you object if I see that for myself?"

He was a doctor, Bridget reminded herself, and

she should treat him as such. She had to school herself to be indifferent to his presence. It wasn't as if she would be alone with him. Molly was in the house, albeit sleeping, but she was there.

"Of course not." Bridget started for the stable door. "She was sleeping when I left."

Jonas followed, switching off the light and making no comment to her last remark. Bridget hadn't expected that it would change his mind, although there had been the possibility it might have.

The sky was purpling into twilight as they walked to the house in silence. An evening star shimmered above the darkening green hills, the pale white of a crescent moon waiting also for night. But the air was still warm from the afternoon's sun. The Vermont dusk was peaceful and serene, but Bridget couldn't match its mood.

"Molly is in the living room lying on the sofa," Bridget said as she walked through the rear entrance of the house ahead of Jonas.

Her over-the-shoulder glance saw his nod of understanding. He said nothing, withdrawing behind what appeared to be a professional mask of aloofness. Bridget led the way through the kitchen into the living room where Molly lay still sleeping on the sofa. Jonas stood above her staring, but made no attempt to waken her.

"Has she complained of anything?" he asked.

"A slight headache. I gave her an aspirin about six hours ago," Bridget admitted.

"Any complaints other than that?" he persisted.

"Like what?" she frowned.

"Dizziness, sharp pains, difficulty focusing her eyes." Absently Jonas listed the possibilities, his attention absorbed in its study of Molly's sleeping face.

"Nothing like that." Bridget shook her head with certainty but felt faintly alarmed.

"Good," he nodded. "I didn't expect she would."

"Should I . . . waken her?"

"There's no need." He ran a hand through his hair, a gesture that implied weariness, and slid a disinterested sideways glance at Bridget. "You wouldn't happen to have any coffee made, would you?"

"I think there's still some from this afternoon, but it would probably be very strong by now," she answered, uncertain whether she should have admitted to having any hot.

"I don't mind. The stronger the better." His mouth curved fleetingly into a smile. "I'd like a cup, if it's no trouble."

"It isn't," Bridget stated with forced politeness.

He followed her into the kitchen, taking a chair at the dinette table while she poured coffee into a stoneware mug. "Cream or sugar?" she offered, carrying the cup to the table.

There was a negative shake of his head to both. "Will you join me?"

How could she refuse? The only other alternative

would be to stand around waiting for him to drink it, and that would only add to the vague sense of unease she was fighting.

"I think I will," Bridget agreed with a stiff smile.

Filling a matching stoneware mug with black coffee, she took a chair opposite him at the table. She cupped her hands around the mug in an attempt to ward off the disturbing chill pervading her limbs.

Jonas sat motionless in his chair, an arm hooked over the back. He seemed withdrawn and distant, his attention absorbed in the black liquid in his mug.

"I owe you an apology, Bridget," he said.

The silence was broken with words that caught Bridget by surprise. She looked at him with startled eyes, but his gaze remained riveted to the coffee mug. A faint furrow of concentration drew his brows together.

"Why?" she asked with a trace of confusion.

"For my behavior today," he breathed in deeply. His mouth tightened in a grim line, but he didn't glance up.

"It's quite all right," Bridget dismissed the need to apologize. She didn't want the conversation between them to be on a personal level.

"No, it isn't," Jonas denied, flashing her a piercing look. "There was no need for me to be so rough with you."

"You explained your reasons before," she insisted coolly, becoming absorbed in the black surface of her own coffee.

"I explained why I asked you to do certain things, not why I was so sharp," he returned.

"It doesn't matter. I've forgotten all about it," Bridget lied and attempted a shrug of indifference.

"Well, I haven't," Jonas refused to let the subject be dropped. "You were naturally concerned about your daughter. You behaved as any mother would have in the circumstances and with considerably less panic than most. I was hard and insensitive to what you were going through."

"It doesn't matter," she repeated.

"Yes, it does," he said roughly. "I shouldn't have let personal emotions interfere and I was angry— angry with you for running from me, the way you have been ever since I came back."

"I wasn't running from you," Bridget corrected smoothly despite the tension coursing through her. "Molly was. I was simply trying to catch her."

"There was no need for her to run from me." There was a fine thread of impatience in his tone. "I wasn't interested in her."

"Molly is aware of that. She senses that you dislike her and responds in the only way she's capable of—by disliking you in return." She met his look, her breath shallowing out at his grim visage.

"It makes it difficult for us, doesn't it?" Jonas murmured.

Immediately Bridget broke away from his compelling gaze. "There is no 'us', Jonas." Trying to conceal that his remark had disturbed her, she picked up the mug, her hand blessedly steady. "Tell me, are you planning to open an office here in Randolph?"

The grooves around his mouth deepened in cynical mockery at her introduction of a different subject. His gaze focused on her lips as she lifted the cup to her mouth. She tried to sip the coffee with an air of nonchalance, denying that his look had any effect on her, and nearly scalded her tongue on the hot liquid.

"I'll be opening a practice, yes," he answered finally, not giving any indication that he had noticed her near mishap. "I've leased a building. The medical equipment and furniture will be installed next week. I've hired a gem called Schultzy to be my nurse, so I'll be opening the office soon."

"Then you are definitely staying," Bridget observed with a sinking sensation.

"Yes, I am definitely staying," Jonas stated with a mocking inflection as if he guessed her unspoken hope. "I made up my mind about that after I saw you in March and Bob told me later that your husband had died."

"You shouldn't have let that influence you," she replied curtly.

"Probably not," he conceded.

"What about your practice in New York? All your Madison Avenue patients?" Unwittingly Bridget had let bitter sarcasm coat her words.

"I worked in a clinic, Bridget," he said, his jaw flexing as if he was exercising control over his anger.

105

"I didn't have a lot of wealthy patients. On the contrary, most of them couldn't afford to be sick. You insist on believing my only interest is money."

Bridget avoided that subject even though she had interjected it by implication. It would ultimately lead to a discussion of the past and arguments and bitterness and all the old hurt. It was difficult enough to endure Jonas's presence without all the old emotions resurfacing.

"Medicine can be costly, as I've learned raising Molly," she smiled, shifting the topic. "I suppose the clinic was sorry to see you leave. Had you worked there long?"

"Since qualifying. I imagine the clinic staff was sorry to see me go, some of them anyway, but they understood that I wanted to have my own practice and get away from the city. They hired a newly qualified doctor in my place."

There was a glitter of impatience in his gray green eyes as if he found the polite conversation a waste of time. His hand, large and well shaped, wrapped itself around the side of his coffee mug.

Bridget searched for a noncommittal response. "There isn't any place quite like Vermont." An inane comment under the circumstances with the air crackling around her, charged with emotional undercurrents she tried desperately to ignore.

"Vermont, hell!" Jonas muttered. "I came back because of you." His hand snaked out to engulf hers before she could pull it out of his reach. "I had to come back to see if we still had a chance together."

The enveloping warmth of his grip burned, flames licking all the way up her arm. It took all of her self-control and resolve not to be swayed by his nearness.

"You're a doctor, Jonas. You save lives," Bridget answered evenly. "But not even you can breathe life into something that died ten years ago." Gently but firmly she drew her hand free of his hold. Rising, she smiled politely. "Would you like some more coffee?" Inside her an earthquake was taking place.

An angry scowl hardened his rugged features, a brooding fire in his eyes as he stared at her silently. Then he pushed his mug toward her.

"Please." The acceptance of her request was issued tautly. "I let it get cold."

Picking up his mug, Bridget walked to the counter where the coffee pot was plugged in. Heat was rising from his cup, but she poured out the contents and added more from the pot.

"It isn't dead for me, Bridget." With cat-soft footsteps, Jonas had approached her from behind. "Is what you once felt for me really dead?" he demanded huskily.

His fingers brushed the chestnut hair away from her neck, their touch against her skin paralyzing her. His hard mouth restamped its brand on the curve of her neck, nibbling at the sensitive cord.

The floor seemed to roll beneath her feet, but it was only the violent trembling of her knees. She swayed for a second against the solid wall of his muscular chest, feeling the promised strength of his arms.

The sensual weakness was momentary. Straightening, she turned, wedging a space between them, and forced the hot mug into his hands. Jonas had no alternative but to take it.

"Your coffee," she declared shakily and took a hasty step away from him.

Her heart was beating so fast it frightened her. Her fingers nervously raked a path through the chestnut hair above her ear. She was being torn apart by the physical and mental conflict going on within. Jonas was still standing by the counter, not moving, watching her intently, gauging her reaction.

"Bridget," his voice was low and insistent.

She had to divert him. "I, er—" she had to breathe in deeply to steady her shaking voice "—I haven't thanked you for what you did today for Molly. Naturally I'll pay for your services. After all, you are a doctor and—"

"Dammit, Bridget! Do you think I want your money?" Jonas hurled angrily, shoving the mug back on the counter.

"I'm the mother of one of your patients. As such I expect to pay for your services," she defended her statement.

His anger was replaced by hardness. "Name my own price, is that it?" he challenged. "Very well." His agreement was as sudden and unexpected as the hand that captured her wrist. "The price is you, and the terms of payment are now."

"No!" Her startled gasp was wasted as he pulled her smoothly into his arms, winding them around her like an iron band.

Bridget strained against his hold, pushing to break free. Mocking complacency curved his mouth as he watched her vain efforts. She was caught fast in the iron jaws of temptation, his muscular thighs burning their imprint on her own. His virile features were unconscionably close.

"Maybe if I'd saved your daughter's life today, you'd be more grateful and more willing to express the fullness of your gratitude," he taunted.

"Let me go!" She was angry—angry and frightened because part of her didn't want him to let her go.

Determinedly she kept her face averted from his. The strong odor of horse liniment was clinging to his jacket. Bridget couldn't avoid inhaling it as his arms made a smaller circle to draw her closer.

The warmth of his breath caressed her skin an instant before his mouth brushed against her temple. Jonas made no attempt to capture her lips, content to explore the winged arch of her brow and her curling eyelashes.

Taking his time, he remapped the familiar territory of her nose and cheek and the lobe of her ear. By the time he was ready to seek her lips, Bridget was trembling with the need to feel the languid passion of his kiss.

Her defenses had crumbled under the slow and steady assault. His mouth closed over hers, tasting the sweetness of her lips. As before his kiss made no demands of her, but when she responded to deepen the kiss, Jonas answered hungrily. The molding pressure of his hands arched her closer to him, crushing her breasts against the hard, metal snaps of his jacket.

The flames of love leaped and spiraled inside her, seeming to join with his to blaze brighter and stronger until she was blinded to all but the primitive desires that drove both of them. His hands slid beneath her blouse to burn over her spine and she felt the growing frustration of not being close enough to him.

When his fingers began tugging impatiently at the buttons of her blouse, she knew a momentary gladness that one of the obstacles would be removed. With a flash of soberness, she also realized where that abandonment would lead. She knew she couldn't do it. She couldn't let Jonas hurt her again and ultimately she would suffer if she gave in to her physical desires, because then she would love him as fully and completely as she had done ten years ago.

Hadn't she learned anything? Hadn't she learned that he couldn't be trusted? He took what he wanted, used it and when something better came along, he walked away. No, no, she wouldn't fall under his spell again, not again.

"No!" Her surrender had been so complete that

Jonas hadn't expected resistance at this late stage.

Bridget twisted out of his embrace, taking three quaking steps before his hands closed around her waist to draw her back. The tormenting need to know his possession was agony. She closed her eyes in an attempt to shut it out, her shoulder blades rigid against his chest.

"You keep saying no while every other part of you says yes," Jonas muttered hoarsely, his mouth moving against her hair.

His hands were spread flat over her churning stomach. Bridget tried to tug them away, without success. His seductive mouth was trailing over the curve of her neck to her shoulder, raising more havoc with her senses.

"The answer is no," she insisted with a choked sob, "I'm not going to let you get to me again. Now let me go!"

Somehow she managed to find the leverage to pry her way free of his arms. This time Jonas didn't pursue her to force her back but stood staring at her. He was breathing heavily, the frustration of anger and desire blazing in his eyes.

Bridget took a wary step backward in retreat, brushing the loose tangle of chestnut hair from her cheek. A fine mist glistened in her eyes from the torment of pain and love. There was a primitive savagery in the hard contours of his features, muscles working convulsively to control it.

"You always did enjoy tearing me inside out,"

Jonas declared in an ominously low voice. "Do you still do that, Bridget? Do you still lead a man on, drive him out of his mind until he doesn't have a sane thought left before you put him out of his misery?"

"Me?" she breathed in hurt protest. "You were the one who did the seducing!"

"You're still trying to protect your righteous and pure image, aren't you, my love?" he jeered, the endearment a sarcastic taunt. "It's slightly tarnished, though, isn't it?"

"Thanks to you! God, how I hate you, Jonas!" Bridget trembled violently.

"Does it make you feel better to blame me?" An eyebrow was lifted arrogantly.

"Yes, it does," she declared. "You took advantage of my youth and inexperience ten years ago. You took what you wanted and got paid for it. Is it any wonder that I detest you?"

"And you were unwilling, weren't you? I forced myself on you, didn't I?" The low angry accusations were issued in rapid-fire succession. "I'm curious, Bridget. How many men have held you in their arms and kissed you and made love to you? How many men have you known since me?"

She stiffened at the assault. "I don't know—I didn't keep count," she retorted coldly. "How many women have you had, Jonas?"

"Why are you avoiding the question?"

"Why are you avoiding mine?" Bridget countered bitterly. "It's always that way, isn't it? You have no right to condemn me for what I have or haven't done in these last ten years. I know one thing—my standards and morals are a lot higher than yours."

"Really?" Jonas taunted savagely. "I'll bet you were a model wife to your late husband. Virtuous as hell! Loyalty, fidelity—you don't even know the meaning of those words. It wouldn't surprise me to find out that your husband didn't even father that eight-year-old girl in the other room!"

A million venomous words swelled her tongue. Not one could find its way out. The palm of her hand struck his lean cheek with a vicious slap, the hard contact shooting needle-sharp pains all the way up her arm.

"Get out!" she hissed.

His gaze narrowed into menacing steel points. The livid outline of her hand marked his cheek; fists were clenched at his side. For a long moment, Jonas stared at the hatred in Bridget's expression, then his long strides were carrying him to the rear door. She closed her eyes as it slammed behind him, the violent action rattling the windows in their frames.

In some way, the slamming door released her own pentup hostility, but the aftereffect was not pleasant. She felt weak and sick to her stomach. A pain more agonizing than she had ever known was strangling her heart. Love-hate, love-hate—she wished she hadn't heard those words in her life.

"Mom?" Molly's drowsy but alarmed voice called out to her.

"I'm—in the kitchen," she answered brittlely, her fingers clutching the counter for support, the knuckles turning white.

"What was that noise?"

Bridget glanced to the door, silent, unable to explain that its closing had awakened Molly. "What noise?" She pretended an ignorance of the cause.

"That loud bang like something exploding."

"Maybe it was the program. How do you feel?"

"Awful," was the grumbling response. "I hurt all over. I'm one big ache!"

That makes two of us, Bridget thought briefly. "What about your head? How does it feel?"

There was a moment's hesitation before Molly answered. "It's sore, but my headache's gone away." Bridget knew a measure of relief at that announcement. "Can I have something cold to drink? My mouth feels like the dentist forgot to take the cotton out of it."

"Iced tea?" Bridget suggested.

"Have we got any lemon?"

"Yes."

"Iced tea with lemon, then," Molly requested.

Bridget attempted a laugh, forced and unnatural. "You can't be feeling too badly if you're still particular about what you are drinking and how it's fixed!"

As she walked to the refrigerator to get the pitcher of tea and a lemon, Molly asked curiously, "Was somebody here?"

With the refrigerator door open, Bridget paused, tensing. "Why do you ask?"

"I thought I remembered hearing you talk to someone in the kitchen while I was sleeping."

A small "Oh?" was all Bridget could manage, fearing her daughter might have overheard some part of the argument with Jonas.

"Maybe I was dreaming," Molly sighed, not quite convinced.

"It could have been Jonas." Bridget filled a glass with tea and sliced a wedge of lemon to add to it.

"Why was he here?" Molly demanded in a contemptuous voice that revealed her intense dislike of him.

Bridget walked into the living room with the tea. "He brought back the horses."

"Did you feed and water the horses for me?" Molly struggled into a sitting position, wincing and gasping at the pain of moving.

"They're all taken care of," Bridget assured her, without identifying who had done it.

"I should go see Satin. She'll wonder what's happened to me." Molly tried to get to her feet, but fell back. "I hurt all over!" she moaned with faint dramatics. "I bet I'll be one big black and blue bruise tomorrow morning!"

"You probably will." Bridget smiled, but her heart wasn't in it.

"Will you help me, mom?" Molly pleaded. "I want to see Satin and make sure she's all right."

"You lie still. Satin is fine."

Instantly Bridget remembered Jonas's comment about a swelling and his suggestion to have her father look at it. She handed the glass of iced tea to her daughter and walked to the phone.

"Who are you calling?" Molly wanted to know.

"Your grandfather."

"Why? Something is the matter with Satin, isn't it?" Molly concluded immediately, her eyes widening in alarm.

"Jonas noticed a slight swelling around her fetlock," Bridget admitted. "He didn't think it was serious, but he suggested your grandfather should look at it."

"What does he know about horses?" Molly discounted his opinion in an emotionally tight voice.

"He's been around them," Bridget answered stiffly, dialing her parent's telephone number.

"If anything happens to Satin," Molly wailed mournfully, "I'll just die!"

Bridget could have told her that when you lose someone you love, you don't die. You keep on living, even if the living is sometimes worse than death. She had first-hand experience, and the sensation was beginning to close around her again.

CHAPTER SEVEN

JONAS STOOD beneath a spreading maple tree on the rockstrewn hillside, an arm braced against the trunk. A haunted look in his gray green eyes, he gazed silently at the steeply sloping roof of the chalet across the meadow below him.

It was the end of July, almost a full month since Molly's accident. He had spent it cursing and despising himself for behaving like such a fool. A doctor was supposed to have some control over his emotions. He should never have lashed out at Bridget with such jealously and anger. But he had wanted to hurt her as deeply as her rejection had hurt him.

He loved her more than he had ten years ago and he wanted to make her love him. It didn't do any good to remind himself that he couldn't 'make' Bridget love him. In his jealous stupidity, he had pushed her the opposite way.

Jonas could make out the slenderly curved form of Bridget taking in the wash from the clothesline in the yard behind the chalet. A tormenting knot twisted his stomach, a hollow ache to touch her and hold her and physically prove that he loved her. Except that wasn't the way.

"Damn!" His fingers dug into the tree bark, totally unmindful of the self-inflicted pain.

Savagely Jonas tore his gaze away from the sight. What had possessed him to buy the land adjoining her parents' farm? He must have been out of his mind. But then he had been since seeing her again. Nothing he'd done had been rational, from selling his partnership in the clinic to buying this land.

He stared at the ground beneath his feet. He was already beginning to wear a path to this tree. The vantage point was only a few hundred yards from his house, giving him an unlimited view of what went on around the chalet. Many an hour he had spent here under the maple, watching, always wishing.

Yes, Jonas had seen her often, but he'd only spoken to her a handful of times. The times when it had been impossible for Bridget to avoid him, the same times he always tried to make happen, with a little luck.

The day after Molly's accident and his abusive words, Jonas had gone over to the chalet. His pretext was excellent—to check Molly's progress. Bridget hadn't let him past the doorway, informing him coldly that their family doctor would look at Molly.

His well-rehearsed apology had not been given a chance to be heard before she closed the door in his face. And Jonas honestly couldn't blame her, although it angered him that she wouldn't even hear him out.

The rare times they had met, on the street or in the

company of mutual friends, the air had been virtually frigid. Invariably his reaction had been emotional, either sardonic with anger or aloof with pride.

The one time he had seen her with Jim Spencer, Jonas had been obsessed by jealousy. He hadn't trusted himself to say a word. In the end, he had left for the nearest bar and got roaring drunk.

His work hadn't helped, although it had occupied countless hours and left him mentally and physically exhausted. That weakened state simply permitted the agony of loving Bridget to take over the other empty hours.

As if drawn by a magnet, his gaze was pulled back to the chalet. He saw Bridget pausing at the door with a basket of clothes in her hands. She lifted a hand and waved. For a leaping instant, he thought she had seen him and his pulse soared.

But no, not at this distance. She didn't have any idea that he kept this lonely vigil beneath the maple tree and it was unlikely that she could see him. His haunted gaze searched for the recipient of that wave and saw the small child cantering a bay mare across the pasture through the dairy herd.

His jaw hardened ominously as he recognized Molly. The child and the gold band on Bridget's finger were both reminders of her past infidelity. Both worked subconsciously on him, feeding the jealous fires that consumed him. In time, there might be something he could do about replacing that wedding ring on her finger. A child couldn't be replaced.

Try as he would, Jonas could not bury his resentment of the young girl. When he looked at her, he didn't see how much she resembled Bridget. He saw her as another man's child, and the knowledge ate at him like a cancer.

Until he found a cure for it, Jonas knew he would never be able to curb the jealousy of another man's loving Bridget. And as long as he let himself be ruled by this jealousy, he could never be the man that she would love. Some day, if he was patient enough, Bridget just might love him.

There was only one chance of a cure. Jonas breathed in grimly and pushed away from the tree. It wasn't to his liking and the odds were that it wouldn't work. But loving Bridget was making him desperate. He would try anything.

Keeping his eye on the horse and rider, he worked his way quietly down the sloping hill. He lost sight of them for a time where the trees grew thicker, but as he neared the pasture fence separating the properties, he saw them again.

He stopped beside a tree a few yards from the fence. He shoved his hands in his pockets and watched the horse and rider approach. There was no longer any trace of the graze on Molly's cheek, although there were a few marks visible on her bare arm. She hadn't seen him and for a moment, Jonas didn't call attention to himself.

The bay mare had seen him. The large, liquid brown eyes studied him. Her head was held high, accenting the arched crest of her neck, her ears alert. The Morgan walked rapidly, displaying an elastic energy that was fully responsive to the commands of her small rider.

Jonas halted his admiration of the mare to glance at the little girl astride it. Molly was sullenly eyeing the No Trespassing sign nailed to a tree near the fence, still several feet from where Jonas stood.

As she drew level with the sign, she stuck out her tongue at it. *Cheeky little brat*, Jonas thought, and immediately reprimanded himself. That was not the attitude to have, not at this moment at any rate.

"The sign doesn't apply to you, Molly," he said in what he hoped was a calm voice.

She reined the bay sharply, glaring at him resentfully for not letting her know of his presence earlier. Jonas saw her reaction and he knew he was responsible for it from the beginning. Perhaps if he had concealed his feelings toward her before—he shrugged inwardly, not finished the thought.

"You're welcome to ride on my land the same as you've done in the past," he told her.

"No, thank you." There was sarcasm in her polite refusal. She laid the reins against the mare's neck to turn her.

"Molly, wait." Jonas walked to the fence.

"Why?" she challenged, checking the mare and eyeing him warily.

"I would like to talk to you." It was difficult to keep the coldness from his voice, to sound warm and friendly, when his head kept pounding that Molly was another man's child.

"About what?" Her small mouth was pulled in a straight line, her chin thrust slightly forward.

Deliberately he shifted his attention to the mare and searched his memory for its name. "Satin seems to have fully recovered from the mishap."

"Yes, she has," Molly patted the sleek neck.

"How are you?"

"I'm fine." She straightened to sit erectly in the saddle. "What did you want to talk to me about?"

Yes, get to the point, Jonas, he prodded himself. But it wasn't easy talking to an eight-year-old, especially one as hostile as Molly. His hand closed over the top of a fence post, absently testing its solidness.

"I have a problem, Molly," he began.

"Do you?" There was a purring note of satisfaction, faintly challenging and spiteful, in her voice.

Irritation flashed briefly in his eyes which he quickly veiled. "Yes, I do. It concerns you. Would you get down so we can talk about it?" It was disconcerting to look up to an eight-year-old.

"Me?" She was doubly wary now. "What do I have to do with your problem?"

"Get down and we'll talk about it," Jonas repeated.

"You don't like me," Molly stated, eyeing him accusingly. "Sometimes you look at me as if you hate me."

He wouldn't have worded it that bluntly. "I know that's the way it seems—"

"It's true," she corrected.

"That's what I want to explain," Jonas replied, exercising extreme patience. "But it's a long, complicated story, so if you would get down off the horse, I'll tell you about it."

Molly hesitated, obviously weighing her curiosity against her reciprocating dislike. Curiosity won as she dismounted and led the Morgan mare to the fence.

She looped the reins around a fence post and hooked her thumbs in the belt loop of her jeans to eye Jonas steadily. It was nearly as disconcerting to look down at the child.

"Let's sit over underneath that tree." He motioned toward one behind him.

Avoiding his intention to help her over the fence, Molly clambered over on her own. She kept a discreet distance between them as if she wasn't sure how much she should trust him. Jonas found her caution vaguely amusing and wise, but it also could prove to be an obstacle.

Molly dropped into a cross-legged position near the tree. She leaned forward to rest her elbows on her knees, all her attention on Jonas as he sat down, waiting for him to begin his story.

"I knew your mother a long time ago," he began.

"Yes, I know. She told me all that," Molly interrupted impatiently.

"What did she tell you?" questioned Jonas.

She considered her answer for a minute, obviously thinking back to the conversation with her mother. "She said you were her boyfriend once and that she thought she loved you. Of course, that was before she met my father." She dismissed any importance of the former.

Dammit—his mouth tightened—don't bring him into it! Not yet anyway. He looked away rather than have Molly accuse him again of looking at her as if he hated her.

"Go on," she prompted expectantly.

Jonas took a calming breath before beginning again. "I loved your mother then, too. I wanted to marry her."

"I'm glad she didn't marry you," Molly declared in a burst of dislike. "I wouldn't want you for a father."

"You never know, Molly," he said, controlling his temper. "I might not be half bad at the job."

She sniffed in contemptuous disbelief and plucked a blade of grass to study it intensely. Jonas was tempted to chuck the whole plan, but he'd already started it so he might as well go through with it.

"As I was saying," he continued, "ten years ago I loved your mother and wanted to marry her. At the time she wanted to marry me. But she was young, barely eighteen, and I still had the rough years of medical school ahead of me."

"You weren't a doctor then?" .

"No, I was just learning to be one." Jonas hestiated, considering his next words. "My family didn't have much money. I always had to work for everything I wanted, including college. Your mother's parents, your grandparents, are fairly wealthy. Bridget had always had just about everything she had ever wanted."

"Is that why you didn't marry her?"

"It was a combination of reasons." He tried to explain. "Your mother said she loved me, but I couldn't be certain how much of what she felt was real and how much was simply romantic dreams because she was so young. And there was the money problem. It isn't easy to watch every penny you spend when you've never done it in your life. Your mother had never had to do that and I doubted that she could."

"I'll bet she could," Molly sighed grimly. "She's always telling me we can't afford something. I want a horse trailer so next year I can take Satin to the shows, but mom says even a used one costs too much money. Grandpa said he'd buy one and let me use it, but she said no." She threw the blade of grass away in disgust.

Admiration flashed through Jonas at Bridget's display of independence. Perhaps he had under-estimated her. Of course, he had to remember that she was ten years older. She had been married, as much as he disliked admitting it, and had to have learned about budgeting and managing.

125

."Plus your grandparents didn't approve of our getting married. They knew it would be several years before I could provide any kind of decent living for your mother, not until I'd qualified as a doctor. And I don't think your grandmother believed I would finish my training."

He and Margaret Harrison had never got along, but Jonas didn't feel it was necessary to go into the psychological reasons behind all that. That was something his maturity and Bridget's could overcome.

"Grandma doesn't like you, either," Molly stated with a suggestion of hauteur. "She wishes there was a way to make you go away again."

"Your grandmother is out of luck this time," Jonas replied dryly.

"You're not going to go away?" she asked hopefully.

"No, I'm not."

Molly sighed in glum resignation, catching the determined tone of his voice. "What does all this have to do with why you don't like me?" she demanded sullenly.

Jonas frowned thoughtfully. "This is the part that's going to be difficult to explain. Or at least, to explain so that you can understand."

"What's to understand?" She lifted her shoulders in an expressively uncaring shrug, but her hazel eyes were faintly anxious when she looked at him.

"If your mother and I had got married ten years

ago, we might have had a little girl like you." He met her look squarely. "Instead I went away and she married your father."

"She loved him." Molly insisted on adding salt to his wounds.

"I know," Jonas snapped harshly. He glanced away, agitatedly running a hand through the hair at the nape of his neck. "Every time I look at you I'm reminded of it and I become jealous. Jealous, because your mother found someone else to love instead of me, because she had his child instead of mine. Do you understand what I'm saying, Molly?"

"I . . . think so," she nodded hesitantly, her eyes wide, as if sensing the unfathomable depth of his emotion.

"Really?" he laughed silently, mockingly skeptical that one so young could have any idea what he was talking about.

"It's not really . . . you don't like . . . ." she faltered as she tried to put into words what she thought he meant. "It's who my father was."

His eyebrow arched in surprise as Jonas studied her more carefully. "You're smarter than I thought," he commented.

"Grandma says I'm too old for my years," Molly said, shrugging.

"Your grandmother doesn't know everything," Jonas pointed out dryly.

"She knows a lot," she defended. "She says you're going to hurt mom again."

"I love Bridget. I wouldn't consciously hurt her."

"Every time anybody mentions your name, mom freezes up," Molly told him. "She doesn't even want grandma to talk about you."

"I hope that some day your mother will care about me again, Molly, I still want to marry her." He ignored her observation.

"She doesn't want to marry you."

"Maybe," Jonas said hopefully. "Maybe it won't always be that way."

"I don't want her to marry you," she said.

"Why? If I could make her happy—"

"You wouldn't want me around," Molly interrupted, again revealing the maturity of her deductive-reasoning prowess, "because I'd still remind you of my father."

"Possibly," he conceded. "But that brings the conversation to the other thing I wanted to talk to you about."

"What's that?" Again she was wary.

"It seems to me that the only chance you and I have to work out this mutual dislike is to get to know one another better," he suggested.

"How would that help?" Plainly skeptical.

Truthfully Jonas wasn't any more convinced than Molly sounded. "I hope that if I learn more about you, I'll realize that you are an individual. That you're Molly O'Shea and not some man's daughter. You might find out that Jonas Concannon isn't a bad guy once you get to know me."

"Do you think so?" Molly frowned, mirroring the doubt she felt.

"It wouldn't be easy." It would be a strenuous exercise in emotional control, considering the fiery passions of jealousy that ran through him each time he looked at the young girl.

"How would we go about doing it?" She wanted to know.

Hell, I don't know! Jonas thought impatiently, but swallowed back the outburst. "I suppose we'd have to get together regularly and talk."

"About what?"

"I don't know." His gaze restlessly swung away from her expression of concentration and demand. The bay mare stamped at a fly buzzing around her legs. "Horses, maybe. The things we like to do and what irritates us."

"You don't know very much about Morgans," Molly stated, harking back to their exchange the day of the accident. "You should go to the Morgan Horse Farm in Weybridge and learn something about them."

"Maybe I'll do that," Jonas agreed patiently.

A sudden twinkle appeared in her eyes. "You can bone up on them." At the blank look, Molly tipped her head to one side, grinning. "Don't you get it? A doctor boning up on something."

"Yes, I get it," he smiled, but the bulk of the smile was turned inward. "I'll 'bone up' on Morgans between now and—say, the day after tomorrow."

Molly paused, unsure. "I don't know. Maybe mom—"

"I don't think you should mention it to your mother," Jonas interrupted.

"You want me to keep it a secret from her?" She frowned.

"I think it's best until we find out if it will work."

She digested his answer slowly. "I suppose you're right," she agreed with reluctance. "But she doesn't like me going anywhere unless I tell her where I'll be."

"You usually ride Satin about this time every day, don't you?" Jonas had seen her out often at this time, but he didn't tell her that.

"It's cooler in the late afternoon, early evening," Molly explained.

"Simply tell your mother that you're going out to ride Satin, which will be partially the truth. You just won't mention that you'll be meeting me." It occurred to him that he was teaching Molly to lie, but it seemed the expedient thing to do.

"Where should I meet you? Here by the fence?"

Jonas glanced across the meadow to the chalet. A meeting here could easily be seen from the chalet. It was entirely possible that if Bridget discovered Molly was seeing him, she would put a stop to it. At this stage, he knew Molly would not disobey her mother to meet him.

"No. Do you see that maple tree in the clearing nearly at the top of the hill?" He pointed behind him to the lookout spot he haunted. Molly craned her neck, then nodded. "I'll meet you there at this same time unless I have an emergency or it's raining."

"Okay," Molly agreed.

In a fluid movement, Jonas rolled to his feet, indicating his desire to end the conversation. Molly stared at him towering above her a second before scrambling to her feet, brushing the leaves from the seat of her jeans. There was a certain anxiety about her expression. Despite her agreement, she seemed to doubt the wisdom of it.

Jonas held out his hand. "Do we have a deal?"

Her small hand was engulfed in the largeness of his as they shook hands to seal their pact. She left it there for a minute to stare at him.

"I may not stop not liking you." Molly seemed to feel honor bound to voice the possibility.

"I might not change the way I feel about you, either," he admitted. "But we won't know if we don't try." And if he didn't try, it could mean Bridget might be lost to him.

"Yeah," she nodded unenthusiastically and withdrew her hand to walk to the fence where the bay was tied.

Jonas didn't attempt to offer her assistance over the fence. Crossing, Molly untied her horse and mounted. She paused to look at him one last time before turning the mare toward the pasture meadow. As they cantered away, Jonas started up the hill, plagued with his own set of doubts.

A few feet short of the maple tree, his appointed meeting place with Molly, he stopped and looked through thickly leaved branches to the steep slopes of the chalet's shingled roof. He wondered what Bridget was doing, and tried to visualize her working around the house. An aching loneliness settled in.

From the kitchen window, Bridget watched Molly cantering the mare toward the horse shed. Her stomach was twisted in knots. What had Molly been talking to Jonas about? It had to have been Jonas. Even at that distance, she would recognize his tall masculine physique.

Her gaze swerved anxiously to the rock and tree-strewn hillside on the other side of the narrow, valley meadow. Jonas had disappeared up the slope. She could see no sign of him anywhere, but it didn't lessen her sensation of unease.

Bridget remembered her mother's warning that Jonas might use Molly to get to her. But she also remembered his resentment and Molly's dislike. There had to be some plausible explanation for their conversation.

Impatiently she walked to the back door, then stopped. No, she shouldn't go charging out to the stables, confronting Molly with the fact that she had seen her talking to Jonas. Her astute daughter would wonder why it was such a big deal, to use Molly's vernacular.

She returned to the sink and began drying the dishes, a task that was normally Molly's chore, but

Bridget needed something to occupy her time. Molly would not be up immediately, since she had to clean the tack, rub down the bay and feed her.

The last pot was in the cupboard when Molly finally walked in the back door. Her sweeping glance saw the draining board empty of clean dishes and she smiled broadly.

"Thanks, mom."

"You're welcome." Bridget tried not to study her too closely. "Did you have a good ride?"

"Sure. Can I have a piece of cake?"

"There's an apple in the refrigerator. Have that instead."

Molly wrinkled her nose and walked to the refrigerator. Bridget lifted the draining board from the sink and put it in the cupboard under the counter. She glanced at her daughter, trying to find a casual way to bring up the subject. There didn't seem to be one.

"Did I see you talking to Jonas?" she asked finally.

"An apple a day keeps the doctor away," Molly recited and laughed as she bit into the red skin.

"Did you talk to him?" Bridget persisted.

"Yes, for a while," Molly admitted in between bites.

"What about?" Bridget held her breath.

Molly shrugged. "He asked whether I was all right and said that Satin looked well. Nothing much, really."

"You seemed to be with him long enough for more than that to be said," Bridget said stiffly.

"He told me it was all right if we rode on his property the way we used to when Mr. Hanson owned it. He said the signs were just there for strangers," she explained.

"I thought you didn't like him."

"I don't, but he is our neighbor," Molly replied. "Plus most of the hilly ground is on his land. Riding over it strengthens Satin's muscles. Jonas isn't such a bad guy, I guess. At least he's stopped talking to me as if I was still an infant."

Munching on her apple, Molly sauntered into the living room. Bridget watched her for a few minutes before turning around to wipe the counter top for the third time. Molly's explanation of the meeting made it sound plausible and innocent enough, yet Bridget couldn't shake off the niggling doubts.

Molly had said that she didn't think Jonas was such a bad guy, even though she claimed to still dislike him. There was a definite softening in her attitude, though. It produced a dilemma for Bridget. She didn't want her daughter to dislike Jonas, but it certainly would make things difficult for her if Molly began liking him.

There was nothing left to do in the kitchen, yet Bridget was reluctant to enter the living room and pretend an unconcern she was far from feeling. Instead she slipped out the rear door of the small chalet, needing some time to be alone.

In the west, the setting sun was splintering pink and gold rays over the green mountains. A serene hush had settled over the valley. The air was still, the temperature cooling. Bridget felt the quiet peace close around her, but it brought no comfort to her troubles.

Bridget wandered to the pasture fence. In the stable, she could hear the rustle of the horses moving around in their stalls, the scent of hay drifting faintly in the air. Black-and-white-spotted Holsteins were grazing in the pasture meadow.

Her gaze swung to the hill rising on the far side of the pasture, Jonas's land. For an instant Bridget thought she saw a flicker of movement near the top. Her heart did a crazy leap as she stared intently, but she could make out nothing. A sigh quivered through her.

Bridget hugged her arms around her stomach to contain the lonely ache she felt inside. "Why did I have to fall in love with you again, Jonas?" She sighed.

CHAPTER EIGHT

"MOLLY," BRIDGET SIGHED in exasperation, "I thought I told you to wear your blue slacks."

"But the white slacks are neater," Molly argued, her mouth curving downward in a rebellious pout.

"They won't be so neat when they're all grass stained. Go up to your room and change before Jim gets here," she ordered.

"Aw, mom!" was the grumbling response. Molly turned to leave the kitchen, then stopped. "How come Jim is taking us to the picnic?"

"Because he asked us to go with him." Bridget added the silverware to the picnic basket.

"Yeah, but he's asked you out a lot lately and you haven't gone with him. How come you decided to go with him this time?"

"Because Jim is leaving," she explained. "He was offered a position at his old college when the man who held it was severely injured in a car accident."

"I thought he was teaching at the Technical College." Molly frowned.

"He was, but he persuaded them to release him from his contract so he could take this other job. In fact, he's already moved. The picnic today is a kind of farewell party for him."

"I thought we were having the picnic because it's Labor Day."

"Okay, Molly, that's enough chatter," Bridget declared, giving her daugher a warning look. "You can talk until Jim comes if you want, but you're still going to have to change those slacks before we leave."

Molly flashed her an angry look and flounced from the room. The half-smile curving Bridget's lips didn't last long as she thought about the coming afternoon picnic. Her first instinct had been to refuse when she learned Jonas had been invited.

It was true that Jonas was barely acquainted with Jim, but he was old friends with the others at the picnic. He couldn't very well have been left out.

Still, it was one thing to meet him on the street or in a store and quite another to see him at an informal gathering like this picnic. Yet living in the same community Bridget couldn't hope to keep avoiding meeting him socially, so she had decided to attend the picnic.

There had been another reason for her acceptance, too. All summer, almost since Jonas's return, she had kept turning down Jim's invitations to go out. It hadn't seemed right to accept them when it was Jonas she secretly wanted to be with.

Bridget knew Jim had been confused by her sudden reversal, but she couldn't explain her reasons to him. She couldn't explain her reasons to anyone. But Jim was leaving and she couldn't turn down his last invitation.

Bridget had stopped kidding herself about Jonas. The ten-year separation hadn't ended her love for him. The only change was that she no longer trusted herself to give that love.

"Forgive and forget," someone wise had once said. But she could not forgive or forget that Jonas had chosen her parents' money instead of her love ten years ago.

A car pulled into the driveway, a horn honking. "Molly!" Bridget called. "It's Jim. Are you ready?"

"Coming!"

The scarlet leaves of the sumac set fire to the roadside. The rusty, cone-shaped seed clusters of the sumac were thrusting upward to the gold sun. Hills and mountainsides were beginning to don their autumn coat of many colors, the red hues of the sugar maple predominant.

It was a scenic drive to Brookfield. The white of a church spire gleamed brilliantly against the background of russet reds and golds of a distant hillside. The closer they came to Allis State Park, the quieter Bridget grew, pretending an absorption in the colorful scenery. Jim pretended not to notice her silence as he responded to Molly's steady stream of talk from her seat between the two of them.

Jim slowed the car as they entered the small community of Brookfield with its cluster of old houses, beautifully preserved. Bridget's tension increased while Molly leaned eagerly forward.

"Are we really going to cross the floating bridge?" she asked.

"We are unless you want to get out and swim across Colt's Pond," Jim teased.

They turned a corner and the floating bridge was at the bottom of the small incline. Buoyed by barrels, it offered passage over the narrow pond.

"We haven't been over this in ages," Molly breathed with excitement.

"Don't wriggle around or you'll capsize us," Jim warned in jest.

The car rolled slowly onto the wooden planks atop the barrels. The bridge took its weight, dipping slightly, permitting water to flow over the boards. The tires made a soft splashing sound as Jim drove slowly across.

At the top of the hill on the opposite side of the pond was the fire tower in Allis State Park. They were among the first of their party to arrive at the picnic area, but the rest soon followed. Bridget kept bracing herself to see Jonas's wagon drive up. Everyone had arrived and there was still no sign of him.

"Where's Jonas?" Evelyn looked around with a frown. "Isn't he here yet?"

"I haven't seen him," someone else replied.

"You talked to him, didn't you, Bob?" Evelyn turned to her husband. "He was coming, wasn't he?"

"That's what he said when I saw him in town the other day," he shrugged.

"I wonder if we should wait for him," Evelyn murmured absently.

"I'm hungry, mom," her youngest complained.

"Let's fix the children's plates," Mary Chapman suggested. "If Jonas isn't here by then, I think the rest of us should go ahead and eat."

"We can save something for Jonas," Evelyn agreed.

The children were called and Molly came rushing up to Bridget. "Do we have to eat with the kids?"

Bridget glanced at the Chapman girl hovering beside her daughter. Both were in fifth grade and certain they were too old to be mixing with younger children.

"You and Patty fix your plates now, but I think it will be all right if you and she find some place by yourselves to eat away from the smaller children." She checked the breathless rush of thanks from the pair by adding, "Check with Patty's mother first. She might want her to watch Tommy."

"We will," Molly promised before they went dashing off.

A few minutes later, Bridget saw the pair stealing quietly away to another picnic table beneath a tree, some distance from the other tables. When all the children had their plates filled and were seated at a table, there was still no sign of Jonas and the adults sat down to eat.

An hour later they were all sitting around the tables, the bulk of the food gone. A car door slammed. Bridget didn't turn around to see who it was. She guessed it was Jonas before the first greeting was called out to him.

"We were beginning to give up on you, Jonas. What kept you?"

He walked to the table. "Sorry I'm late."

"We saved some food for you," Evelyn smiled.

"Thanks," Jonas smiled tiredly.

Bridget couldn't help noticing his crumpled appearance. His print shirt and brown trousers both looked as though they'd been slept in. His hair looked as if it had been combed with his fingers. His features seemed leaner, darkened by a shadowy beard growth. There were haggard lines etched around his mouth.

"From the looks of you, you must have been at one helluva party last night," Bob observed in jest.

"It was no party," Jonas replied, sliding his long legs under the picnic table and sitting down with obvious weariness. "A maternity case."

"Who had their baby?" Mary Chapman asked.

"No one from around here." He shook his head. "A young couple had come up from Massachusetts to spend the holiday weekend at Lake Champagne. She went into labor about one in the morning. I was on call at the hospital."

"What did she have?"

"A girl." He made an effort to smile, but it

141

couldn't reach his eyes. He glanced at Bob. "You don't happen to have any beer left?"

"I think there's a couple of cans left in the cooler." Bob winked.

"What would you like to eat?" Evelyn asked. "We have—"

"I'll take a couple of those hot dogs. That's good enough," Jonas insisted.

His gaze slid to Bridget, then skipped to Jim sitting beside her, but there was no outward reaction, except a kind of resignation. Bob sat a can of beer in front of him and Evelyn passed him some hot dogs and chips. The conversation became general again.

Jonas had finished the first hot dog and picked up the second when the blare of a horn sounded. He breathed in deeply and set the sandwich on the paper plate.

"Excuse me," he said, rising tiredly to his feet and stepping over the picnic-table bench.

He walked to his car as the horn blared a second time. Bridget watched him discreetly, her heart strings being tugged by his lack of vitality, something that had always been so much a part of him. Leaving the car door open, he sat sideways in the driver's seat. A second later she saw him with the receiver of a mobile phone in his hand.

"Let's start clearing up this mess," Connie suggested as she pushed up the sleeves of her sweater.

"We'll get out of your way," Bob laughed.

"You could help," Evelyn told him.

"We could," he admitted and grinned as he and the rest of the men hastily retreated from the tables, leaving the women to clear the food away.

Jonas returned a few minutes later, wearily rubbing his forehead. The plate with his food had been left on the table, but he didn't walk back to it. Instead he wandered to where the men had gathered and leaned a shoulder against a tree a few feet away, a part of them yet aloof.

"Bridget," Evelyn spoke quietly, looking at Jonas with faint concern, "why don't you take his plate over to him? He doesn't look as if he's had a decent meal in days."

Bridget agreed, but she hardly wanted to be the one to point it out to him. She hesitated for a second, unable to find an adequate reason to refuse. Finally she nodded and picked up the plate, walking quietly over to where he stood.

"Jonas," she murmured his name, and he turned. His gray green eyes looked at her, yet seemed to look absently right through her. She held out the plate. "You didn't finish."

He glanced at it and looked away. "I'm not hungry."

"I admit it doesn't look to appetizing now. The meat is cold, but you really should eat something," Bridget persisted in a determinedly calm tone.

"Probably," he agreed indifferently and rubbed a hand over the stubble on his jaw and chin. "I forgot to shave." He mused the discovery aloud.

"You also forgot to eat. Please, Jonas." She offered the plate to him.

His gaze shifted to meet hers, held it for a second, then looked at the plate. Straightening from the tree, he took the plate from her hand. Bridget waited, guessing that the moment she turned her back he would set it down or dump it in the nearest garbage can. He eyed the sandwich, then unexpectedly and roughly shoved the plate back in her hands.

"Jonas—" Bridget started to protest.

"I lost the baby," he declared in a low, angry voice.

"Oh!" she breathed in sharply.

"She was premature, an ounce over two pounds," he explained gruffly. "We did everything. We had all the best equipment, but we couldn't save her."

Bridget could sense his frustration, his feeling of helplessness when he felt he should have been able to do something. She wanted desperately to offer him some kind of comfort.

I'm sure you did everything you could, Jonas." The trite phrase came automatically to her lips.

"Yes." His mouth twisted cynically as he continued staring off into space. "But it wasn't enough, was it?" he murmured rhetorically. Breathing in deeply, he closed his eyes for a tired second. When they opened, the brilliant fire in his gaze was focused on her. "I had to tell someone. I don't know, for the life of me, why I chose you. You don't care."

His words were a stinging slap, the pain intensified

by the step he took away from her. Her fingers touched his forearm to stop him.

"That isn't true, Jonas," she denied tightly. "I do care."

He studied her upturned face. "Yes, but not the way I mean. Excuse me." And he walked away from her light hold.

Bridget watched him join the men and saw him refuse Bob's offer of another can of beer. There was a lump in her throat as she walked back to the picnic tables. She swallowed it hurriedly at Evelyn's frowning look.

"He wouldn't eat?" she asked.

Bridget shook her head. "He said he wasn't hungry and I couldn't persuade him he should eat anyway." She guessed that Jonas didn't want the party spirit dampened with the explanation for his brooding mood and kept silent about the loss of the baby.

Bridget helped the women with the rest of the clearing up, but her gaze kept straying to Jonas. He looked exhausted, yet he didn't sit down. Always he was standing or wandering around. Bridget was certain it wasn't a restlessness that drove him but a fear that to relax would bring sleep. And Jonas was denying himself the luxury of rest.

The impulse was strong to seek him out again and persuade him to go and get the sleep he so obviously needed. Her previous attempt to get him to take needed nourishment had been summarily rejected.

Another expression of concern for his welfare would undoubtedly meet with the same result.

When the picnic tables were cleared and the baskets returned to the cars, the women began to join the group of men. It was as if Jonas sensed the exact moment that Bridget started toward the men. At her approach, he strolled with seemingly aimless intent away from them. Automatically Bridget slowed her steps to see where he went, stopping when she saw him heading for the tree where Molly was sitting with Patty Chapman listening to a portable radio. Engrossed in their chatter, they didn't see or hear his approach. All of Bridget's senses were attuned to him and she gravitated a few feet closer.

She saw him come up on them from behind and reach down to turn the volume knob lower. Both girls started in surprise, looking up with alarm.

"Don't you girls think that radio is too loud?" His gray green eyes crinkled with a smile. "The next thing you know, you'll be treated for deafness!"

"Jonas!"

Molly's squeal of delight at seeing him stunned Bridget. She stared at the trio in shocked disbelief. The last time she had questioned Molly about Jonas, her daughter had sworn she disliked him, but that had been a month ago or more.

Molly's attitude was anything but hostile. Bridget tried to regret the change of heart, but couldn't. In fact, there was a certain warm satisfaction in seeing them together like that.

"Gosh, you look tired, Jonas," Molly declared with concern.

"I look that bad, do I?" A halfsmile curved his mouth, affectionate and indulgent. There wasn't even a glimmer of his previous resentment of Molly.

"What happened?" Molly asked.

"No sleep," he answered. "I had an emergency call from the hospital last night. I just came from there straight to here."

"An emergency? I suppose it was some horrible automobile crash." Molly focused all her attention on him, her hazel eyes widening.

"Sometimes, Molly, you have a very morbid curiosity," Jonas chuckled.

"Teachers always tell you that if you don't ask questions you don't learn anything," Molly declared importantly. "Who knows? Maybe I'll decide to be a doctor when I go to college. Just think of the head start I could have by learning all about it from you first."

Bridget stared, the full implication of the conversation beginning to hit her. There was confusion and a vague sense of unease. Jonas squatted beside the two girls.

"I was over by Weybridge the other day," he said. "I had a couple of hours to spare, so I stopped by the Morgan Horse Farm run by the college."

"What did you think of it?" Molly asked, eager for his opinion.

"I was impressed."

"It's grand, isn't it, with all those gorgeous Morgans, and the stallions are magnificent. And the beautiful old buildings," Molly enthused.

"Considering your obsession with Morgans, I'm surprised you don't want to attend the training course at the farm," Jonas observed.

"Oh, I do. I'd love to, but—" Molly lifted her hands expressively "—it's so hard trying to figure out what you're going to do when you get older."

"I think you have plenty of time to make up your mind," he replied dryly.

"I suppose so." Molly sighed and leaned back with a pensive look in her eyes. "I wish I could have visited the farm with you. It's been so long since I was there."

Only a year, if Bridget remembered correctly, but her attention was concentrated on the rapport between the man and the girl. It was such a natural exchange, something that couldn't have happened overnight.

"Maybe I—" Jonas stopped, his gaze slicing to where Bridget stood listening. A hard mask stole immediately over his rugged features, concealing the warmth that had softened them only a moment ago. "Maybe your mother will take you," he changed his response and straightened.

Frowning at his sudden change, Molly followed the direction of his narrowed gaze to Bridget. Guilt flashed across Molly's face, replaced by anxious dismay as she glanced back to Jonas. The line of his mouth seemed to become grimmer, and slow, purposeful strides carried him to Bridget.

Jonas stopped in front of her. "I suppose you want an explanation."

Bridget felt the catapulting of her heart and a crazy weakness in her knees. There was also a slow, burning anger that he could confront her so calmly.

"I believe I'm entitled to one," she answered stiffly.

His gaze swung to the picnic group and Bridget's did likewise. No one seemed to have noticed them together or were even looking in their direction.

"Let's walk," Jonas suggested.

"Very well," Bridget agreed. She, too, preferred that their conversation should be private without the risk of someone overhearing.

Jointly they turned and walked away from the others. A subdued Molly watched them go, her eyes round and apprehensive. A thin layer of fallen leaves carpeted the grass beneath their feet, making a soft rustling sound as they walked.

When they reached an area fairly secluded from the others, Jonas stopped. He reached into his pocket for a cigarette, lit it and offered it to Bridget. She refused it with a shake of her head and waited expectantly for Jonas to begin.

He inhaled deeply on the cigarette and blew out a thin trail of smoke. The action seemed to accent the tired, strained lines etched around his mouth and eyes. But Bridget refused to give in to the wave of compassion. As the seconds stretched, so did her nerves.

Finally Jonas said, "I confess I've been seeing Molly."

"For how long?" Bridget demanded.

"A month. More than that. Since the end of July," he admitted after a second's consideration of the length of time.

"Why, Jonas?" Her hands were clasped tightly together. She stared at the pattern of bark on a tree rather than look at him.

"I wanted to get to know her. It seemed the logical way."

"But you made certain I didn't know about it," she accused.

"I didn't think you would approve."

Bridget darted him an angry glance, but a wispy cloud of smoke curling from the cigarette veiled the look in his eyes. The rest of his expression was unreadable.

"You were quite right about that," she agreed. "I wouldn't have approved. And I suppose you encouraged Molly not to tell me about your clandestine meetings."

"If you knew, they wouldn't be a secret. And I guessed you would put a stop to them once you found out. Yes," Jonas admitted, "I suggested to Molly that she shouldn't mention them to you."

"I suppose you met while she was out riding?" At his nod, Bridget looked away. "You actually encouraged Molly to deceive me. That was an under-handed thing to do, Jonas."

"Probably," he conceded. "But if I'd been straightforward about my intentions, you would have seen to it that I didn't succeed."

"You actually believe you were justified. I don't know why I'm so surprised," she laughed bitterly. "You always did take what you wanted regardless of who was hurt. You always believed you were right and justified. Now you do something underhanded like this. No, I shouldn't be surprised."

"You're overreacting, Bridget," Jonas said patiently.

"Am I?" she challenged.

"I hope you don't blame Molly for it. It was entirely my idea." He ignored her challenge.

"I'm aware of that."

"Good," he nodded, "because Molly was insistent that you always knew where she was. The only thing she kept from you was that she was meeting me while she was taking her rides."

"It was still a deception," Bridget insisted, then faced him in agitation. "Why did you do it, Jonas? What did you hope to gain?"

"I told you—I wanted to get to know Molly." He levelly returned her intent look.

"Yes, but why? I suppose you were going to have Molly persuade me to change my opinion of you in your favor. She's a child, Jonas," Bridget's voice trembled huskily. "Do you think I would let her influence me? She has no idea at all how ruthless you can be and I do. You surely didn't believe I would listen to her, so why? Why did you do it?"

Jonas didn't answer immediately. He took a last drag of the cigarette and dropped it to the ground, grinding it out beneath his heel and exhaling twin streams of smoke from his nose. Bridget held her breath, feeling the coiled tension in him.

"I was very close to hating your daughter, Bridget." He spoke quietly and distinctly. "It's a symptom of a disease known as jealousy, and it was getting out of hand. Every time I saw Molly or was reminded of her or saw that wedding ring on your finger, it consumed me, goading me into saying things to you I didn't mean."

"If that's the way you felt toward her then—" she began stiffly.

"—Why did I make arrangements to see her?" Jonas finished the question for her, his mouth twisting wryly. There was a sardonic glitter in his eyes. "You've probably already come up with an answer for that. But you're wrong. It wasn't to get her into trouble with you, to have the two of you exchange harsh words over me."

Bridget paled at the accuracy of his guess. "Then why?"

"I didn't resent her because she was your daughter. It was because she was 'his' daughter. The only cure seemed to be not seeing her as anyone's daughter, but as a person, an individual."

"From what I saw a moment ago, you appear to have succeeded." Nervously she moistened her lips, her voice brittle.

Part of her wanted to believe that his motives were as altruistic as he claimed, but there were too many doubts from the past for Bridget to trust his explanation.

"We have a friendship of sorts. I have no intention of using it against you, Bridget," Jonas stated.

"Don't you?" she mocked skeptically, knowing its existence had already given him an advantage she didn't want him to have.

Jonas reached out, taking her lightly by the shoulders and turning her to face him. "I don't want Molly getting dragged between us. She isn't going to be a pawn. I hope I've pushed her out of harm's way so that regardless of the outcome between you and me she won't be hurt by it. I don't want her hating either of us."

The touch of his hands made Bridget suddenly and very acutely conscious of him. Her skipping heart was blinding her to all the reasons she shouldn't respond to him. She stood unresisting beneath his light hold.

"But don't think I've given up, Bridget," Jonas continued, his darkening gaze roaming possessively over her upturned face, "because I haven't. I still want you and I still love you. Maybe some things have changed, but that hasn't. There are some things you just can't forget."

His head bent to lightly claim her lips, mobilely exploring them while he gently drew Bridget into the circle of his arms. It was a languid fire he kindled but a warming one just the same. If time could stand still, Bridget would have been content to let that moment stretch for an eternity, bathed by the radiant light of her love.

When he raised his head, the satisfying warmth of his kiss fled. Bridget was once again chilled, her mind taking over control from her heart.

"I haven't forgotten," she said coolly. "In fact, there are some things I remember more vividly than you do. Like the way you left."

"You were young, Bridget." Jonas sounded weary. "You were young and spoiled by your parents, and I had a lot of years of school ahead of me. I explained why I didn't want to marry you then when I left."

"And I might have believed you," Bridget smiled with melancholy bitterness, "if I hadn't known about the money."

He breathed in deeply and emitted a short cynical laugh as he let his arms slide loose of their circle around her. "I once tried to convince myself that I'd hurt you very badly when I left and that you'd married your husband on the rebound. Do you remember what else I told you that day I left ten years ago?" he asked. At Bridget's wary frown of blankness, he answered the question. "I told you I would come back. But you married your husband after I left. The truth is, Bridget, if you'd really loved me ten years ago, you would have waited for me. And that's something I haven't forgotten, although, Lord knows, I've tried."

She stared at him, feeling a pain so sharp that she couldn't open her mouth to confirm or deny his statement. It paralyzed her. She could neither move nor speak. A whole new set of doubts assailed her at the view she had seen from his side.

Jonas held her gaze for several more seconds before glancing at his watch. "Excuse me—" withdrawn and indifferent now "—I have to be at the hospital at four."

Pivoting, he walked toward his station wagon. Bridget pressed a finger against the center of her forehead, the pain of confusion pounding at her head. He had sounded so sincere, but she was afraid to believe him.

"Mom!"

Bridget turned, fighting her way through the bewildering maze of conflicting thoughts to smile brittlely at the young girl hurrying toward her. Molly's expression was a mixture of anxiety and guilt.

"Did Jonas tell you?" she asked fearfully.

For an instant Bridget forgot how her conversation with Jonas had begun and she was wary when she replied, "Tell me what?"

"About my meeting him up on the hill whenever I went riding," Molly explained almost as if she was unsure whether she should admit in case Jonas hadn't told her.

"Yes, he told me," Bridget nodded.

"I'm sorry, mom. I should have told you, but—" Her daughter was reluctant to put into her words exactly why she hadn't.

"I know why you didn't. Jonas was certain that I wouldn't approve," Bridget made the explanation for her.

"Was he right?" Molly breathed anxiously.

It was Bridget's turn to hesitate. "No," she said finally.

"You mean you don't mind if I meet him now and then?" Molly returned with surprise.

"No, I don't mind," Bridget answered stiffly. "But don't keep it a secret from me any more. That was wrong."

"I won't," Molly promised, then added on a slightly fervent note, "He is kinda nice, mom, once you get to know him."

"Yes, I know." Bridget wanted to warn her daughter not to become too fond of him, but she couldn't.

She couldn't take her own advice. Besides, she wasn't certain any more if the warning was necessary.

CHAPTER NINE

AUTUMN'S FIRE had begun to spread through the hills with more leaves changing to the brilliant fall colors. Only the evergreens remained immune to change, staying darkly green, nature's accent for the others.

From the kitchen window, Bridget stared at the hills, not seeing their steady change to autumn's glory. She was thinking of the man who lived in the farmhouse hidden by the nearest hill. She was thinking of Jonas.

Since their conversation at the picnic almost three weeks ago, he had occupied her thoughts almost exclusively. His statement had given rise to a whole new set of questions that plagued Bridget because of her inability to find the answers. They were answers only Jonas could give.

She had seen him half a dozen times in the last three weeks, talked to him on each of the occasions, but there had always been others around. Jonas hadn't suggested, invited, nor asked to speak to her alone. And Bridget had been hesitant to take the initiative.

Until she knew the answers, she was beginning to realize that the wondering would drive her insane.

She would have to forget her pride or her upbringing, whichever it was that stopped her, and make the first move.

Bridget glanced at the telephone mounted on the kitchen wall and immediately dismissed its use as the way. She wanted to see Jonas's face when he answered the questions. There was only one way to do that.

For the first time in years, she obeyed an impulse. Taking her car coat from the closet, she slipped it on as she hurried out to the car and drove out of the driveway onto the road.

The tires spun uselessly in the gravel for a second before finding traction. The small car shot forward. After three weeks of waiting, Bridget was overcome by the need for haste. Within minutes, she had covered the semicircular route to the farmhouse.

The engine had barely died when Bridget stepped out of the car and walked swiftly toward the rear entrance. Her knock on the door didn't bring any answer and she knocked louder, with the same results.

There was always the possibility that Jonas was on the telephone and couldn't come to the door. His station wagon was parked in the driveway, so he had to be here.

She tested the doorknob and found the door unlocked. She pushed it open and walked into a silent house. She hesitated in the kitchen, listening and looking at the empty rooms, empty of Jonas at any rate.

"Jonas?" she called. "Jonas?"

The rear door of the house opened behind her and Bridget turned with a jerk, her heart leaping at the sight of Jonas striding toward her. A confused frown darkened the angular planes of his face.

"Bridget," he said her name as if he couldn't believe his eyes. "When I saw you leave, I never expected you to come here. What's wrong?"

Relief washed through her at finding him. Soon all her questions would be answered and she would finally know if she had been misjudging him for ten long years.

"Oh, Jonas, I'm so glad you're here," she declared weakly.

He misinterpreted the reason for her statement. His expression became grim as he gripped her shoulders firmly, his gray green eyes boring into her, a faint professional mask stealing over his face.

"Is it Molly? Has something happened to her?" he demanded, giving Bridget a brief shake as if thinking she was giving way to panic.

"No, no, Molly's fine," she assured him with a tremulous laugh of relief.

"Then why—" A wary confusion glittered in his look.

"I had to see you," Bridget explained with an aching throb in her voice.

"Why? What about?" Jonas demanded, then groaned at the faint glow of love in her hazel eyes. "I don't give a damn why you're here!"

His fingers curled into her chestnut hair, lifting her head to meet his descending mouth. There was an explosion, flames leaping within Bridget at the searing fire in his kiss. Her hands curved inside his fleece-lined parka and around his waist, feeling his muscles straining to press her closer.

Gladly, she tried to oblige. Her toes barely touched the floor as she arched against him, his length taking her weight and the hard circle of his arms providing support. The male scent of him was an aphrodisiac to her senses, drugging them with an erotic nectar.

His driving hunger was insatiable. Sensually he devoured her lips, nibbling, tasting, exploring, never getting his fill. The furious hammering of his heart was as loud as her own, thudding in her ears with a wild tempo.

Slowly he let her feet touch the floor, bending her slightly backward over his arm. He began diversionary tactics to completely undermine her self-control, exploring the curve of her cheek, the delicate and sensitive lobe of her ear and the pulsing vein in her neck.

His searching, caressing hands pushed at her car coat, its bulk interfering with his desire to touch her. Bridget aided his attempt to remove it, letting it slip to the floor. Then her own hands tugged at his parka until Jonas discarded it.

It was done in one fluid movement that ended with Bridget being lifted off her feet into his arms.

Automatically she wrapped her arms around his neck, glorying in the male strength that carried her weight so easily. His gaze burned over her love-soft face before his mouth sought her eager lips again.

The living-room sofa was his objective, sitting on it with Bridget across his lap. His hands arousingly caressed her waist and hips, gliding down her thigh and back again. Every inch of her felt on fire, a molten mass of desire, her flesh pliant to any of his demands. She wound her fingers into the luxurious thickness of his golden brown hair.

"I've waited so long for this moment," Jonas declared in a throaty murmur against her cheek, pressing hard kisses on her smooth skin. "To hold you like this again."

He lifted his head to look at her, desire blazing in his half-closed eyes. What breath she had was stolen by that searing look.

"I know," she softly echoed his sentiment.

Her fingers began a tactile exploration of the lean, ruggedly hewn features she loved. They traced the jutting curve of his cheekbone and lightly stroked the hard angle of his jawline to his chin. From there, her fingertips outlined the firm male curves of his mouth, trembling slightly as he kissed them.

Then his head was bending her toward her again, seeking the hollow of her throat. "This makes all the waiting and watching worthwhile." As he spoke, the warmth of his breath sent dancing shivers over the skin of her neck.

"Watching? You were watching me?" Bridget murmured with absent curiosity.

Her hands slid down the tanned column of his neck to the open collar of his shirt. She fingered the buttons, loosening them from the material to splay her hands over his rough-haired chest, warming them with the body heat radiating from his hard flesh.

"From the hill behind the house," Jonas admitted, nuzzling her collarbone. "Like a lovesick puppy."

His mouth trailed slowly up her neck to her soft lips, closing moistly over them, forcing them apart, although they needed little persuasion. His weight pressed her backward onto the seat cushion of the sofa. Jonas shifted so that he was half lying beside her and half above her, their legs entwining.

There was seductive mastery in his deepening kisses, yet their passion was a languourous thing as if each wanted to savor the soaring joy of the moment. Bridget trembled as he unfastened the buttons of her blouse and slid his hand inside to cup the mature fullness of her breast enclosed in a lacy bra.

Disentangling his lips from her mouth, Jonas directed their attention to the exposed swell of her breasts and the tantalizing cleft between them. Bridget shuddered at the intimate contact, her desire leaping at the dizzying caress.

"Where's Molly?" Jonas asked huskily.

"Molly?" She felt completely disorientated by his heady nearness.

"Yes. Is she home? God, I hope she doesn't expect you back soon," he groaned achingly and buried his mouth along the curve of her neck, becoming entangled in her silken chestnut hair.

"No, she's at a . . . party." Bridget caught at her breath as he located the sensual pleasure point near the nape of her neck. "A—a birthday party for one of her friends."

"What time do you have to pick her up?" Jonas demanded thickly.

"I don't," she answered and felt the rigidity leave his muscles.

"Is someone bringing her home?" he asked with almost absent interest, concentrating again on arousing a sensual excitement in her.

"No, she's—" Bridget paused as he succeeded in sidetracking her thoughts.

"She's what?"

"She's spending the night with Vicki," she finally managed the answer.

"You're spending the night, too," Jonas declared huskily, "with me."

The blunt statement acted as a brake to Bridget's previously unchecked desire. When he would have again claimed possession of her lips, her fingers lightly pressed themselves against his mouth to stop him.

"Jonas, wait," she begged.

"That's all I've done since I came back." He stared darkly into her face, trying to fathom her sudden hesitancy when she had displayed such open willingness seconds before. "I love you, Bridget."

"I believe that," she said and had to swallow the catch in her voice. "I love you, too, but—" she admitted what she hadn't been able to deny to herself.

"But what?" Jonas frowned, his compellingly handsome face only inches above her own. "My God, it isn't as if it's the first time!"

"It isn't that," she insisted.

"Then what is it?"

"There are some questions I wanted to ask before—" Bridget faltered and left the rest unsaid. "That's why I came over tonight."

Jonas looked away, his eyes closing as he exhaled a long breath. With suppressed anger, he levered himself upright away from her and savagely rubbed the back of his neck.

She watched silently, knowing he was angry with her. She was upset with herself for letting his embrace make her forget the reason for her visit. Unexpectedly he rose from the sofa and started to walk from the room.

"Where are you going?" Bridget frowned in confusion.

"To get some coffee," Jonas snapped, not hiding his irritation or frustration behind any mask of calm. "If this is going to be another one of our typical word exchanges, I'll need to sober up and get my wits about me."

His disappearance into the kitchen was followed by the slamming of cupboard doors and the clanging of cups on saucers. Shakily Bridget pushed herself into a sitting position on the sofa as the impatient tread of footsteps signaled his return.

A glance at the hard set of his features, uncompromising and grim, made Bridget regret again that she had allowed his first kisses to sidetrack her from her purpose. The small tray in his hands held two cups of coffee. He set it on the low table in front of the sofa and took one of the cups.

"I poured you some coffee." With the clipped announcement, Jonas sat down in an armchair opposite the sofa as if needing distance between them.

Bridget picked up the remaining cup, hoping the black coffee would steady her nerves. She held it with both hands, trying to ward off the pervading chill that had suddenly enveloped the room.

"All right, what are your questions?" he demanded, breathing out heavily in an attempt for patience and control.

"It's about—the money." Bridget stared at her coffee, unable to meet his piercing regard.

"The money," Jonas snapped in irritation. "It always comes back to that, doesn't it?"

"Yes," she nodded, wondering why he couldn't understand the way his selling out had plagued her all these years.

"Whenever you run out of things to accuse me of,

you always chase back to that." He sipped at his coffee without appearing to notice that the liquid was scalding hot.

"It should be obvious to you why I do," Bridget retorted in agitation.

"No, dammit! It isn't," Jonas retorted.

"What if the roles had been reversed?" she argued. "What if your parents had offered me money? What if I had taken it and left? What would you have thought of me for doing that? Is it something you could forget—something you would overlook and then welcome me back with open arms ten years later?"

"No, I couldn't," he answered harshly. "But then that wasn't exactly the case, was it?"

"Wasn't it?" Bridget countered. "Isn't that what you did to me?"

"You know the circumstances were entirely different." His cup was returned to its saucer with a decided clink.

"They were not!" She, too, cast her cup aside to rise in agitation. "You took the money and left."

"Yes, I took the money and yes, I left." Jonas would have gone on, but Bridget interrupted him.

"How can you say it was different?" she accused.

"Because it was! I told you I loved you and was coming back." His voice was low and tightly controlled, as if he was determined not to turn it into a shouting match.

"Yes, you loved me." Bridget laughed bitterly in

disbelief. "That's why I received so many letters from you, I suppose," she taunted. "I didn't get one, Jonas, in case your memory has failed you on this point, too. Not a single, solitary one! You left Randolph ten years ago, telling me you loved me and promising to come back. But you left with a lot of money in your pocket—my parents paid you to leave. Why should I have believed that you were coming back? Not when you didn't even write me!"

"You know damned well that was one of the conditions your parents attached to the money," Jonas declared savagely.

"Conditions? What conditions?" she hurled back. "They asked you to leave me and leave town!"

His gaze narrowed sharply, a sudden angry watchfulness to his expression. "There was more than that, Bridget."

"What?" she challenged with a toss of her head, clasping her arms in front of her and absently kneading her elbows in nervousness.

"Part of the agreement was that I should make no attempt to contact you for six months, neither in person, by phone, or by letter," he answered.

"No?" Bridget frowned in questioning denial.

"Oh, yes," Jonas nodded with certainty, a harsh glitter in his look. "You mother wasn't convinced that you really loved me. She believed you were too young for marriage, something that I was more than half convinced about myself. It was her decree that there be six months of absolutely no contact between us. Supposedly after six months if we still felt the same, she wouldn't stand in our way."

"She said that?" she breathed.

"And you didn't know about it?" An eyebrow quirked in a suggestion of mockery.

"I didn't."

"That's possible," Jonas conceded with a disgruntled sigh.

"But after the six months, why didn't you try to see me? Why did you wait for so many years?" Bridget ran a hand through her chestnut hair in confusion, believing him yet not fully understanding.

"You're forgetting something this time," he taunted cynically. "Maybe I wasn't in direct contact with you, but I did stay in touch with some of our friends. Within a couple of months after I left Vermont, you did, too. By the end of six months, there were rumors that you'd married or were marrying someone else. Which you did, didn't you, Mrs. O'Shea?"

"Jonas, I—" she began.

"So what was the point of my trying to get in touch with you? Your mother had proved that she'd been right. You couldn't have loved me or you would have waited. You were too young to make that kind of commitment," he stated in a hard, flat voice, "probably even to your late husband, but he conveniently died before that could be proved."

"That isn't true." But Bridget didn't want to explain about Brian yet. "Everything you say sounds so reasonable, but there is one thing you haven't explained to me."

Jonas leaned back in his chair in a relaxed attitude, yet his eyes were sharply alert and his mouth grim. Bridget wished there was no more to talk about. She wished she could be in his arms.

But, until these questions were out of the way, she knew that no matter how much she loved him, she would never be able to completely trust him. The doubts had to be eliminated or confirmed.

"What is that?" he asked with forced patience.

She faced him. "Why did you take the money?"

He exhaled a short, silent laugh and shook his head. "The way you say the word always makes it sound like blood money!"

"That's what it feels like," Bridget replied in a low, hurt voice. "You sold me out. You sold our love out. Even if I'd waited for you. Even if I'd known about the six-month's condition, there was still the money you took. It was a lot more than thirty pieces of silver."

"Dammit, Bridget, it wasn't a bounty!" Jonas pushed out of the chair, towering in front of her in a momentary rage that he quickly controlled, although it seethed below the surface. "Or even a gift."

"Well, what do you call it?" she breathed in painful anger. "You've obviously had time in the last ten years to come up with a pat explanation for it."

"No, I have no pat explanation for it," he declared in an ominously low tone. "Only the truth."

"Which is?"

"The money was a loan."

"A loan?" Bridget laughed bitterly, and turned away to stare at the ceiling. "Can't you come up with something better than that?"

"It's the truth." Her shoulders were seized and she was spun around to meet his piercing gaze. "You have to know how much medical school costs. I admit that when your parents offered to loan me the money, it was essentially a bribe, but as far as I was concerned it was an investment in our future, yours and mine. I never expected you to meet some man and marry him less than six months later, even though I knew it was a possibility. But the money was still a loan."

"Is that true?" Bridget frowned.

Jonas released her shoulders in a gesture of disgust. "I paid it back, Bridget."

"What?" she breathed.

"I was lucky," he told her with a trace of irony. "I managed to obtain a couple of grants and didn't have to use it all. I repaid the loan in full two years ago, before I knew you were widowed."

"You paid it back?"

"Yes. Now I suppose you'll claim that I did it because I had a guilty conscience about accepting the money in the first place." Jonas turned away with a shake of his head.

For ten long years Bridget had believed she knew all the details surrounding his leaving. Now she realized that she hadn't—only what her parents had told her. There were a lot of things they had failed to tell her, it seemed.

A cold chill ran down her spine. "You are telling the truth." It was a statement.

"Don't take my word for it." Jonas slashed a cutting look over his shoulder.

"I—" Bridget was about to deny the need for that.

But Jonas interrupted, "I mean it, Bridget. Don't accept what I say. Ask your parents. As a suggestion, if I were you, I'd ask your father: I'm not certain your mother would be capable of giving you an unbiased answer."

"But I—"

"Go home," he said firmly. "Go home and ask them."

Bridget stared at his wide shoulders. Her heart was filled with an aching love that was boundless. She wanted to touch him, to somehow show him how deeply she cared.

"I believe you, Jonas," she said in a soft, throbbing whisper. "I don't need my parents to confirm your story."

"I want them to confirm it." He pivoted to face her. The line of his jaw revealed his unyielding stand. "When you come to me, Bridget, when you marry me, I don't want there to be any room in your heart for doubts. None. Not about you and not about me."

She wanted to protest, to argue, but his hard, short kiss silenced the attempt. She swayed toward him.

He broke it off, but he held her firmly at arm's length.

"Go home, Bridget," he ordered and gave her a little push toward the rear door.

Bridget left, not because Jonas had ordered her to leave, but because he was right. No matter how much faith she had in his word, there would always be the chance of doubts surfacing some time later unless she rid herself of them now, for good.

The instant she walked into the chalet, she went straight to the telephone and dialed her parents' number. Jonas had been right about another thing: her father could be trusted to give her an unvarnished account, without prejudice.

If she had stopped at the house, the chances were that she would not have been able to speak to her father in private. By telephone, she could persuade him to come to the chalet under one pretext or another.

Her mother answered the telephone. "Is dad there?" Bridget asked.

"No, he's gone to an auction. He probably won't be home until late. Why? Is something wrong?"

"No, nothing," she assured her mother quickly. "Why are you calling?"

"I heard about a used horse van that was for sale," Bridget lied. "The price sounded reasonable and I was going to ask dad if he would mind looking at it for me. I'll talk to him tomorrow about it."

"I'll mention it to him. Molly does have her heart set on one, doesn't she?" her mother commented.

172

"Yes, she does," she agreed.

It was nearly twenty minutes later before Bridget was able to end the conversation with her talkative mother.

With getting Molly off to school in the mornings, working at the shop all day herself and trying to elude both her daughter and her mother in the evenings, it was four days later before Bridget had a chance to speak to her father. He confirmed everything Jonas had told her, as she had guessed.

After trying three times unsuccessfully to reach Jonas at his home, Bridget finally gave up and waited until the following day to call him at his office from her shop. The phone rang several times before his nurse answered.

"I'd like to speak to Dr. Cancannon," Bridget requested.

"Did you wish to make an appointment?" was the crisply professional reply.

"No, I would just like to speak to the doctor."

"Regarding what? Are you one of our patients?"

"No. It's a personal matter," Bridget explained.

"He's with a patient. Let me see if he can take your call now. Who's calling, please?"

"Bridget O'Shea."

"Oh!" The nurse's voice immediately became bright and cheerful. "Of course he'll take your call. Just give me a minute to pull the stethoscope out of his ear and hand him the phone. He'll be right with you. Hold the line."

Bridget waited, anxiously watching the shop door, hoping she would have no customers until she had spoken to Jonas. There was a vague fluttering of her heart as she realized that nothing stood between her and Jonas any longer. They could be together.

"Hello, Bridget."

His voice, when he answered the phone, was calm and level, as though he saw nothing momentous in the occasion, while Bridget was suddenly all nervous and jittery.

"Jonas!" she spoke his name in glad relief. "I phoned to tell you I talked to my father last night in private."

"And?"

"And he told me exactly what you had."

"Good," Jonas said decisively.

"When I think of the things I said to you and what I thought all these years, I—"

"There's no need to apologize," he interrupted smoothly. "You weren't in possession of all the facts. I should have put you straight in the beginning. You aren't to be blamed for misunderstanding the situation."

"Maybe not, but I—" But that wasn't important anymore. "When will I see you, Jonas?" she asked boldly.

"I'll be attending a convention this weekend, so I'll be out of town." He sounded so distant. "Let's make it a week from Saturday."

"So long?" Bridget frowned. "Jonas, what's wrong?"

"Nothing is wrong." Then he hesitated. "Bridget, I want to have time to think—very seriously about us. We've waited more than ten years. We can wait more than a week."

"I love you, Jonas," she said.

"Tell me that next Saturday."

Bridget could almost hear the half-smile in his voice as he rang off. It was only after the line was dead that she remembered it was Molly's birthday a week from Saturday and she had promised her a party.

It was hardly the circumstances Bridget would have chosen for their final reunion, but she let the arrangement stand. After all, Molly and her friends wouldn't require constant chaperons on the scene at all times.

CHAPTER TEN

"THE CAKE is going to be beautiful, mom!" Molly declared in a loud stage whisper as she bent over the counter to get a better look.

"It won't be if you don't get out of my light," Bridget warned.

Dutifully Molly leaned back as Bridget added the finishing touches, outlining the circumference of the cake with blue frosting. There was only the outside base left. Bridget paused to add more blue frosting to the decorator tube.

"Can I put the candles on now?" Molly asked.

"Wait until I'm through," Bridget answered, hiding a smile at the impatience of her daughter.

She had barely begun squeezing the blue spiral from the tube when there was a loud knock at the door. The suddenness of it made Bridget squeeze the tube too hard, sending out a glob of frosting. She cursed beneath her breath and reached for the knife.

"See who it is, Molly," Bridget ordered and started to repair the damage to the cake.

"It might be Kathy. She was going to bring over some records for the party." Molly skipped to the rear-entrance door in the kitchen.

"Why would she bring them now?" Bridget frowned.

"Kathy and Vicki were going to come early so they could help make the pizza," Molly informed her as she opened the back door. "Jonas!" she cried in delight.

Bridget pivoted sharply to the door as he walked in. He looked rugged and manly, fresh from the mountains in a dark suede parka lined with fleece.

Her stomach somersaulted and she felt terribly weak at the knees. Then she became conscious of Molly eyeing her apprehensively, nibbling at her lower lip as if uncertain whether Jonas would be welcome.

"It feels like snow outside," Jonas declared, shutting the door behind him.

Bridget's gaze flickered to the gray sky outdoors. She tried to respond calmly. "This is the first week of October. The snow probably won't be too far away."

"That's true." His gaze ran over her from head to toe.

"I didn't expect you so soon." Bridget became conscious of her appearance.

She had wanted to change and put on fresh makeup before he arrived. She brushed the hair away from her forehead with the back of her hand, forgetting about the frosting-coated knife she held and smearing the blue icing on her cheek.

"You were expecting Jonas?" Molly breathed in surprise.

"Didn't I mention to you that he was coming over?" Bridget set the knife down, knowing very well she hadn't said anything to Molly because she hadn't wanted to make a lot of explanations yet. Taking a damp towel, she wiped the frosting from her cheek that was not slightly tinged with embarrassed pink. "Although I had thought it would be later tonight. I haven't had a chance to clean up."

"You look fine," Jonas assured her, yet there was a certain reserve in his voice as if he was masking his feelings.

"You always look great, mom," Molly added her endorsement, but it didn't carry the same weight as his.

"I suppose I should apologize for coming early, but I remembered Molly mentioning that today was her birthday." His arm moved to reveal the ribbon-wrapped package he had been holding behind his back.

"For me!" Molly shrieked.

"Do you know anybody else in this house who has a birthday today?" Jonas teased and handed it to her.

"Can I open it now?" Molly asked Bridget, clutching the package excitedly.

"Go ahead," Jonas said, and Bridget nodded her agreement with his answer.

With painstaking care, Molly slid the bright ribbons from around the gift-wrapped box, her hazel eyes sparkling with ecstatic pleasure. Bridget's were nearly misted over with tears. The paper was removed with equal care before Molly lifted the lid of the box to see what was inside.

"A saddle blanket!" she cried with delight.

"Careful," Jonas warned when she started to lift it out. "There might be something else wrapped up in it."

Molly's eyes widened curiously before she set about unfolding the bright blue blanket. The thick material kept Bridget from seeing what was inside, but she did see the frown that suddenly appeared on her daughter's face. Just as suddenly Molly started laughing.

"What is it?" Bridget asked, overcome with curiosity.

"A doll!" Molly declared, lifting a china-faced doll from the blanket's folds.

"I thought every girl should have one whether she was too old to play with them or not," Jonas stated, his mouth twitching in a smile.

"It's terrific!" Molly grinned. "Both presents are terrific! Thank you, Jonas."

"You're welcome." He inclined his head briefly, smiling, the corners of his eyes crinkling.

The telephone rang. "I'll get it!" said Molly.

"Answer it in the living room," Bridget told her and Molly darted into the other room.

A second later the ringing stopped and Molly called back, "It's for me!"

Slowly Jonas crossed the room to where Bridget

stood. His gaze flicked briefly to the nearly decorated cake. "It looks nice," he observed.

"I forgot to tell you Molly is having a party tonight. A half a dozen of her school friends are coming over," she explained, wishing he would discard that mask so she could see what he was thinking.

"For how long?"

"All night. Molly is having a slumber party. I've been promising her she could have them over for a long time."

"You're kidding." Laughter gleamed in his eyes.

"No, I'm not," Bridget smiled faintly.

He was standing close to her. She had to move only slightly to touch him, but somehow it didn't seem necessary. Bridget had the deliriously warm sensation that he was already holding her in his arms and loving her.

"Have you changed your mind?" he murmured, his compelling gray green eyes holding her gaze.

"About what?" she asked, feeling the sensual pull of his attraction.

"About me," he answered. "You've had over a week to think about whether or not you want to marry me. Whether you really love me."

"I've loved you for more than ten years, Jonas," Bridget answered with amazing calm. "A week hasn't changed that."

His hands spanned the sides of her waist to draw her to him. Bridget melted willingly into his arms, lifting her head for his kiss. It was a searing sweet promise of love, laced with passion and stamped with a hint of possession.

More than at any other time that Jonas had held her, Bridget felt that she had come home. She was safe and secure. He loved and needed her as much as she did him.

"I love you, Bridget." Jonas made the declaration in a hoarsely fervent tone, lifting his head only inches above hers.

"I love you." She returned the vow. Her hands were resting on his shoulders. She was about to wind them around his neck when she noticed the cake decorating tube she still held and the swirling glob of blue frosting on the dark suede of his jacket. "Look what I've done to your coat!" she exclaimed with a rueful laugh. "I'll clean it off."

Twisting out of his arms, she set the decorating tube on the counter where it couldn't do any more damage and reached for the damp hand towel. Jonas watched her with a lazy smile as she vigorously wiped at the blue mark.

"That's enough," he stated after a few seconds and shrugged out of his coat to toss it on the nearest kitchen chair.

"I didn't get it all," Bridget protested.

"I don't care." Jonas shook his head briefly and curved his arms around her, locking them together at the small of her back. "Besides, I feel like a birthday cake—all gay and bright and on fire."

The light in his eyes gave Bridget the same feeling. He bent his head toward hers, brushing his lips over her cheek and temple. The musky fragrance of his aftershave lotion combined with his male scent to fill her senses with heady results. His body heat made her think she was standing in front of a roaring fire.

"We'll be married next week," he told her, his mouth moving against her smooth skin as he spoke. "As soon as I can arrange it with the minister. Is that all right?"

"Yes," she breathed.

"Will you have time to do everything? We're going to have a real wedding, Bridget, with as many trimmings as time will permit. It isn't going to be any rushed, hole-in-the-corner ceremony. I love you and I want everyone to know it."

"Of course there'll be enough time." Every second hectic and frantic, but Bridget knew she wouldn't want to change it. The smile faded from her lips as other, more serious thoughts crowded their way to the front. "Jonas, I want to tell you about Brian and my mar—"

"No." His hand covered her mouth to stop the words and stayed there. "This last week I've had time to do some soul-searching. During the ten years, nearly eleven, that we've been apart, a lot happened to each of us. I don't want you to explain anything to me about your late husband or your marriage. It's none of my business. Our life together starts from this moment, and that's all that counts."

"But, Jonas, there's—"

"I know," he interrupted. "There's Molly to be considered. I like her, Bridget. She's an amazing person." Bridget noticed that he didn't make any comparisons, likening Molly to her or her father. "After we're married, I'd like to legally adopt her if you and Molly agree."

"I think both Molly and I would," Bridget nodded, "but, Jonas, I want to tell—"

"We aren't going to talk about the past any more, only our future," he insisted firmly.

"Jonas," she declared with an indulgent and faintly exasperated smile, "count the candles Molly had laid out for her cake, there, on the counter."

"What?" he frowned bewilderedly at the request.

"Count them," Bridget repeated.

Still frowning, Jonas glanced at the candles laid out in a row beside the cake. "Ten white ones and one blue one." The furrow across his forehead deepened as his questioning swung back to Bridget. "What's the point?"

"Molly is ten years old today. The blue candle is to grow on," she explained.

"Ten?" His gaze narrowed on her smiling face.

"Molly is your daughter, Jonas." Bridget stated the obvious with loving patience.

"What?" He stared at her uncertainly.

"Do you remember—" her fingers began smoothing the collar of his shirt, a caressing quality in their movement "—that Saturday we started out to go skiing cross country and happened across that abandoned logging camp? We went inside one of the huts to get warm and—"

His arms tightened fiercely around her. "Do you honestly think I've forgotten the first time we made love?" he demanded huskily. "We spent the whole day there. The sun was going down when we left. We barely got back before dark."

"Less than a month later, you left. A couple of weeks after you had gone, I realized I was going to have your baby."

"Why didn't you let me know?" he groaned.

"How?" Bridget reasoned without any bitterness. "You never told me where you were going or how I could reach you. As far as I was concerned, you'd deserted me. When you took my parents' money and left, I was convinced you'd sold out your right to know about our baby. She was mine alone."

Jonas turned away from her in agitation, raking a hand through his hair. "I should have considered the possibilities," he growled in self-accusation. "I should have known. No wonder you hated me when I came back!"

"It wasn't easy, because I still loved you," she told him quietly.

"Your pregnancy was the reason you left Vermont after I did," he concluded.

"Yes. When I told my parents, mother arranged for me to stay with her sister in Pennsylvania," Bridget explained.

"This Brian, your late husband, I remember you told me that he was gentle and understanding. He must have been to marry you and be the father to another man's child. I understand why you cared for him so much," Jonas sighed heavily, rubbing the back of his neck.

"Brian—" she hesitated "—Brian O'Shea didn't exist."

"What?" Pivoting, Jonas confronted her with a piercing look.

"He was a figment of my mother's imagination. She wanted me to give the baby up for adoption once it was born, but I couldn't do it. And my mother—well, she didn't want it known that I had a baby out of marriage. So she came up with phony papers and marriage certificates to prove I was married. I went along with it because I felt a certain amount of shame, too." She breathed in deeply, staring at the gold wedding ring on her finger, another symbol of the farce that had been perpetuated. "And I didn't want you to know about Molly. I wanted to be able to say she was another man's baby if you ever came back. I was afraid you would feel responsible or want to marry me because of her. I didn't want you that way."

"Bridget." His arms wrapped around her, hugging her close and rocking her gently as if to belatedly ease the pain and anguish she had gone through alone. "I love you. At least you know I wanted to marry you because I love you before I found out about Molly. If it's possible I love you even more now that I know."

"I'm glad." But it was a small word to describe the wild elation throbbing inside her as she snuggled against him.

"I still can't believe it," Jonas breathed against her hair. "I know it's late, but inside I'm bursting with pride. I feel like passing out cigars. I have a child. We have a daughter!"

Bridget lifted her head to look up at him. Her breath was caught by the brilliant mist shimmering in his eyes and the wondrous smile illuminating his face. "Yes, we have a daughter," she agreed, her voice choked with emotion. "Molly doesn't know, of course, but we'll tell her."

"Together," Jonas promised. A flicker of concern crossed his features. "Do you think she'll mind?"

"We'll explain everything," Bridget said. "She's old enough to understand. She likes you, too, Jonas. It might take her some time to adjust, but I know she'll love you eventually and be proud to be your daughter."

"Old enough?" he laughed silently. "You told me she was eight years old going on nine. And I believed you, even though there were times when I thought she was overly mature in her attitudes. No wonder!"

His mouth was teasing the corner of her lips. Bridget moved to seek his kiss, knowing he understood the reason for her deception about Molly and didn't mind.

"Have you finished the cake, mom?" The question that started out in a rush slowed quickly when Molly rounded the archway into the kitchen and saw the embracing couple. She stopped, wide-eyed, as the two glanced at her.

"Come on in, Molly," Jonas invited, unlocking his arms from around Bridget.

"I was going to put the candles on the cake," Molly explained uncertainly.

"I'll have it finished in a minute." Bridget turned to the counter picking up the decorating tube.

"Yes, mother," Jonas mocked playfully, "you'd better get that cake decorated for this young lady's birthday."

Molly walked over, watching both of them curiously. Jonas leaned a hip against the counter to watch Bridget add the blue base to the cake. He dipped a finger into the frosting bowl.

Bridget lightly rapped his hand. "Stay out of there!"

"You have all you need, don't you?" Jonas countered.

"Yes, but—"

"Come on, Molly, you and I are going to lick the bowl." He picked it up from the counter. "Bring a couple of spoons.

Taking two spoons from the silverware drawer, Molly followed him laughingly to the kitchen table. Bridget watched, forgetting the cake for the moment. Their chairs were pulled close together, both heads bent over the frosting bowl. One was chestnut colored and the other was tobacco gold.

They were a family. All three of them together. There might be other happier minutes than this in her life, Bridget knew, but this scene would live forever in her heart.

What the press says about Harlequin romance fiction...

Take these
4 best-selling novels
FREE